MY TRUST IN YOU

THE SUMMER UNPLUGGED EPILOGUES BOOK 2

AMY SPARLING

AMY SPARLING

ONE

IT'S wild how fast time goes when you aren't paying attention. It seems like just yesterday my son was being born, and now he's about to start kindergarten. My mom used to complain that my brother and me were growing up too fast, and I always thought she was just messing around. But she's right. Kids grow too fast.

I park in front of Lawson Elementary School, where the big yellow banner standing in the grass reads: *Register your student today!* I knew Jett would start school this coming year, but I seeing that sign when I drove by the other day was like a shock to my system. It's time to register him for school. This is all happening so fast!

"What is this place?" Jett asks from the backseat of my SUV.

I turn around, grinning at him. "It's your school."

He makes a face as he stares out the window. "I don't want to go to school. I want to stay home with you and Daddy and ride dirt bikes!"

"You'll still get to ride dirt bikes," I say. "But every kid has to go to school. It's how you get smart."

"I'm already smart!" he protests.

I chuckle to myself as I get him out of his booster seat and hold his hand as we walk up to the front of the school. I see a few parents coming and going, but no kids, which is weird because this is a school, even if it is in the summertime.

All of Jett's concerns about going to school seem to evaporate when we walk in the front doors. The school is so cool inside. The walls are lined with colorful murals, and the library, which is off to the left, has literal plastic tube slides going from the second floor down to the first floor. It's filled with books and plush bean bag chairs and looks like a paradise for children's books.

"I want to go to school!" Jett says, squeezing my hand, his eyes wide with awe as he looks around.

"You'll get to start school in a couple weeks," I tell him.

At the front office, I wait for the older lady behind the counter to acknowledge me. She's busy typing on her computer and taking papers from the printer, but finally, she looks up.

"Can I help you?" Her hair is pulled in a tight bun on top of her head and she peers at me over the top of dark blue frame glasses.

"I need to register my son," I say, feeling weirdly scrutinized for some reason.

"Okay, where's your confirmation print out?"

"My... what?"

She heaves a sigh. "You have to register him online, then print out your confirmation sheet and bring it here."

"Oh, sorry. I didn't know." They could have helped out clueless parents a bit by writing it on the banner outside.

Another woman walks into the office, paper in hand. Then two more parents arrive, each with papers. I guess *they* knew how to register online. I guess all the other parents actually know what they're doing in life and not just winging it like I am. I feel like an idiot as I walk Jett back to the car.

"Does this mean I don't get to go to school?" he asks, frowning.

"No, it just means your mom is dumb."

"Mommy's not dumb," he says, smiling up at me, his messy dirty blond hair all in his eyes.

I smile at him, grateful for the compliment even though he's wrong. How did I not know how to register my own kid? This is something I should have looked up online before just showing up at the school. Maybe I should have asked my mom for help, but I've been trying really hard to be independent and not like some loser who has no business being a parent.

When we get home, it's time for lunch so I make Jett and me peanut butter and jelly sandwiches with Cheetos and grapes before digging my laptop out from under a pile of clean laundry on the couch and looking up the school's website. Sure enough, there's a registration link on the home page, which takes me to a Google form. Jett runs around the living room, toy dirt bike in his hand, while I work on the form. I fill out all of his information, and all of my information, along with Jace's name, email, and phone number too.

After I submit the form, it tells me to bring Jett's

birth certificate and vaccination records to the school to finalize his registration. My eyes widen. Ah, crap. Paperwork.

I look up and across the living room. Sure, Jett has paperwork. Somewhere. All of our paperwork is tucked away in boxes somewhere in the house. When Jace and I moved from our apartment into the new home we had built, we just kind of dumped all the boxes in the spare room. And the dining room. And upstairs. I have all my stuff from my childhood bedroom at my mom's house in boxes, and Jace has all his stuff from before he met me in boxes, and we have all our old stuff from our apartment, too.

Most of the furniture and kitchen accessories and stuff were all either bought new for the house, or given to us as housewarming gifts. I haven't dug through those old moving boxes in a couple of years. With a sigh, I close my laptop and set it on the coffee table. Then, seeing Jett's toys all over the place, along with smudges of grape jelly from his lunch, I think better of it and move the laptop to my bedroom. It was expensive, and I don't want it to be a casualty of my wild five-year-old.

Leaving Jett to play with his dirt bike toys and

watch cartoons on the TV, I walk into the spare bedroom and face my fear: moving boxes.

There are so many of them!

How do we have so much stuff? And what's worse, is that when I packed up stuff, I just scribbled nonsense on the boxes. I should have made a detailed list of everything that was inside, but instead I wrote "stuff" on a dozen boxes. "Bayleigh" on others. "Jace's junk" on some. It's ridiculous.

I try peeling back the packing tape from one box marked "baby" and break my fingernail in the process. Wincing in pain, I retreat out to the kitchen in search of a box cutter. Luckily, our kitchen junk drawer has plenty of odds and ends, including a box cutter. I head back upstairs and eagerly cut open the box. Surely his box labeled "baby" means it contains Jett's baby paperwork.

Only, it doesn't. The box is full of baby clothes. Before I know it, I've wasted half an hour pulling out each little tiny baby outfit and remembering how sweet and precious Jett looked while wearing them so many years ago. The nostalgia hits me hard. After tucking all the clothes back into the box, I open several more but none of them have Jett's paperwork.

"Mo-ommmm," Jett calls out in that voice that means something is wrong.

I rush out and find him standing in the kitchen, face turned down bashfully.

"What's wrong, honey?"

"I'm thirsty."

"Okay, let's get you a drink."

"I already tried that," he says.

I open the fridge and gasp in horror. What was once a pitcher of Kool-Aid is now red liquid all over the inside of my fridge, drowning all the food inside.

"What happened?"

Tears spring to his eyes. "I didn't want to bother you so I tried getting it myself."

"Son, you need to get my help for stuff like this. You're never bothering me, I promise."

"I'm sorry."

"It's okay, honey."

I lose track of how much time it takes me to clean out the fridge, but it must be at least an hour because Jace is home before I know it. He walks in through the back door, wearing jeans and a black T-shirt with The Track's logo on the front. He's been working outside on a dirt bike track in the sun all day and yet he still looks like a movie star and I look like a frumpy weirdo with a messy bun and Kool-Aid-stained clothes.

"What happened here?" Jace asks, taking in the sight of the empty fridge and all the fridge contents sitting on the kitchen table.

"Oh, just another wonderful day in the life of being a mom," I say, standing up and wrapping my arms around him. He smells like the woodsy outdoors mixed with a bit of motor oil.

Jace chuckles and kisses me on the forehead. "How'd kindergarten registration go?"

I heave a sigh. "What if we just don't send him to school and let him be a wild heathen child instead?"

Jace cocks an eyebrow. "Huh?"

I shrug. "I can't find his birth certificate and I need it for the school."

"It's in the safe," he says.

My mouth falls open. I totally forgot about the safe. "It is?"

"Yup." He grabs a protein shake from the stack of fridge stuff on the table and cracks open the lid. "Along with our birth certificates and marriage license and stuff. I keep all the important paperwork in the safe in our closet."

"What would I do without you?" I say as relief floods into my sore muscles.

"You'd be fine without me," he says with a grin. "But you wouldn't have an amazing, talented, super cute kid without me."

I roll my eyes. "You mean the kid that's currently coloring on the walls?"

TWO

SINCE NONE of the other parents had kids with them when I went to the school yesterday, I decide to leave Jett at our business childcare center with Deja today. Deja is incredible with the kids she watches and Jett loves her. I feel bad leaving him, but without him in my car I can blast my music without worrying about it hurting his ears. I make a lot of sacrifices to be a mom, and I don't regret any of them because my son is the best kid ever, but it's fun to have a little alone time every so often. I work at The Track, the motocross business Jace and I co-own with our best friends Park and Becca, and The Track has a childcare center in it, so even though he'll hang out in the childcare room while I'm working, I've still been with Jett for every day of his entire life.

Now that he's starting kindergarten, I'm a little worried that I won't know what to do without him with me for seven hours a day. But I'm also a little eager for the time as well. I'll be able to work harder at The Track and help turn it into an even better business which will become a legacy that Jett takes over one day. Still, I'm going to miss my little wild child while he's at school.

Armed with my registration paperwork and Jett's official documents, I head back inside the school to finish enrolling him. Only this time, there are a dozen parents in line and they all brought their kids with them. What the heck? No one had a kid with them when we came here yesterday.

I step in line, which trails out of the front office and into the hallway. Several minutes pass and I don't move up in the line, so I take out my phone and scroll through social media. My personal accounts are set to private because the public can be really nasty to me. Many of Jace's motocross fangirls are resentful that I'm the one who got to marry him, and they'll probably never get over it. Because I only have close friends and family members on my Instagram, I post a lot of family photos. Nothing fancy, just little bits of my life.

But on The Track's official social media profiles, I work really hard to make our business look professional and also trendy. I take photos from all angles, showcasing our track and the nice facilities. Jace and Park are basically celebrities around here, so every time I post a picture of them, we get thousands more likes and comments.

I scroll through the pictures I've taken over the last few days and find one of Jace posing shirtless, wearing just his motocross pants and boots, pointing at the vending machine. He looks gorgeous, and he's promoting a great protein drink company.

Back when we opened the business, Jace's mom Julie wanted to help out by investing in the business. Jace didn't want her to because he wanted to do it all himself, an even fifty-fifty split with his best friend, Park. But Julie insisted that it would just make her happy to help out somehow. So she bought three industrial vending machines for our front office. We buy drinks and snacks at wholesale prices and sell them for a dollar, so in Julie's small way, she found a way to help make our business earn more profit.

A few days ago, Jace met Ricky Brant, who is also a young entrepreneur. He created the Braap Protein energy drinks that are healthy and delicious, and Jace decided to stock them in our vending machines. I select the picture and add it to The Track's social media account, letting everyone know that we now have Braap Protein on site.

The line moves forward slowly. People's kids scream and yell and run all over the place. One little boy even gets mad when he runs up to the library and tugs on the door only to find it locked. He drops to the floor and starts screaming and crying because he wants to go play on the slide. His mom just ignores him, her attention on her phone. I feel embarrassed for her. Who does that? Jett would never run around and kick and scream in a public place. I've raised him better than that, which is saying something because sometimes I think I have no idea what I'm doing.

At least I know better than to let my kid ransack a school because he's not getting his way.

The line slowly moves forward again. I text my best friend Becca and tell her how boring it is, and she replies that it's also slow at work right now so it's not like I'd be having fun if I were there.

I step forward one more spot in line and take a deep breath. Waiting in line is boring.

"Excuse me."

The soft, friendly voice comes from behind me. I'm not even sure she's talking to me, but when I glance back, she smiles at me. She's probably in her late thirties. A pretty woman with light skin, lots of makeup, brown hair that looks like it was professionally styled in a salon, and a really cute outfit. Her toes are painted purple and her nails are manicured, and she's even wearing jewelry that matches her shirt.

I don't know a lot about designer brands, but it's obvious that the handbag dangling from her arm is one of the expensive ones. Here I am in flip flops, yoga pants, a baggy T-shirt, and no purse because I left it in my car and shoved my car keys into the side pocket on my leggings.

"Hello," I say when it's obvious she is talking to me.

"Are you a nanny?" She flashes me a bright white smile. "I've been looking forever to for a good nanny to watch my kids while my husband and I go on vacation."

"No, sorry," I say, wondering where she got that idea.

"Oh, you must be a big sister then? Are you interested in nannying?"

"I'm a mom," I say. "I'm here to enroll my kid, and I can't be a nanny, sorry. I have a full time job."

Her eyes widen and then she laughs. "You can't be serious! You're just a baby yourself."

Some people say things like that in a rude way, hinting that I must be some kind of tramp for being such a young mother. But she doesn't seem like she's that kind of person. I think she's just surprised and can't keep her mouth shut and says whatever comes to mind first.

"I'm older than I look." This phrase has become my go-to response when people say I look young.

"Well in that case I'm sorry for assuming you were the nanny. I've just been so desperate to find a nanny that I'm asking every young woman I come across if she happens to be one." She holds out her hand. "I'm Elle."

"Bayleigh," I say, shaking her hand.

"You don't happen to know a nanny, do you?"

I laugh. "No, sorry."

"Ah well," she says with a wave of her hand. "My search continues."

We move forward in line again. "So is this your first kid?"

I nod. "First and only."

"Do you want more?"

"I'm not sure yet," I say honestly. People always ask if I want more kids and I really don't know. I've got enough on my plate with just the one kid, but maybe one day that will change.

"I have four," Elle says. "Today I'm enrolling my youngest."

"Wow, four kids? How do you find time to look so amazing?"

She laughs and pats her slim belly. "Lots and lots of exercise."

I didn't mean her figure... I meant all of her. How does this woman function with four children and still manage to get dressed up and do her hair and makeup? She must be some kind of wonder woman. I only have Jett and I barely manage to wash my hair every few days, much less style it.

We move forward in line again, and soon I'm being summoned to the front desk to finish my registration. When Elle waves goodbye to me, I notice a keychain hanging from her wrist. It's one of those bracelet keychains, all fancy with rhinestones and charms dangling from it. I notice the social media tag @LawsonMomLife hanging from her keychain, followed by her name.

It's a cute keychain, but I'd never reveal my social media publicly like that. Too many weirdos out there.

THREE

OUR BUSINESS HAS SETTLED into a groove that makes my life fun and fulfilling. Becca and I work up front at the Track, scheduling clients, answering calls, and keeping everything running. Jace and Park give motocross lessons to help riders of all ages get better at the sport. We also have a gym on site since the guys wanted one to easily be able to work out each day, and we turned it into a membership opportunity to earn even more money. Lawson is a fairly small town so a public gym was totally needed.

On work days when it's not too busy, I try to duck out an hour early and get a workout in. I'm not in incredible shape or anything—not even close to Jace's fit body—but I enjoy the endorphins and the fun cardio break in my otherwise lazy day that involves sitting at the front office. But today I plan to skip the gym and head out early to do school supply shopping for Jett.

Becca squeals from across the room. We're both in the front office, but she's sitting behind the counter on the work computer and I'm making another cup of coffee, because every day around two in the afternoon I get a caffeine craving I can't resist.

"What is it?" I ask.

She smiles at me and claps her hands together once. "I found a new T-shirt supplier. They have good quality shirts and they're made here in Texas, and they cost two dollars less per shirt than the other place we were using."

"Nice!" I give her an air high five by holding up my hand from across the room. We started selling shirts with our business logo on it a few months back and they sell out quickly. People love them, especially since we donate half the profits to a local charity that helps the homeless.

"So are you going school supply shopping tomorrow?" she asks while I'm stirring sugar into my coffee.

"No, I'm going at three today so I can beat the

traffic." We only have one Target within an hour drive and it's always super busy during rush hour. You have to go early in the day if you want to avoid some of the craziness.

"Um…" Becca says, flattening her lips like she's about to tell me bad news. "It's three-thirty."

"What!" I turn my wrist to check the time, because I had an alarm set to remind me for today, but my smartwatch is dead. Probably because I forgot to charge it, because I seem to forget everything lately. I curse under my breath and leave the coffee I just lovingly made in front of Becca. "You can have this. I gotta go."

"Bye," she calls out, snorting to herself as I rush down the hallway toward the childcare room to get Jett.

We race across town—well, as fast as I feel safe driving over the speed limit which is only five miles an hour over—and then end up parking at the back of the lot because the store is packed. It's "back to school" season so the stores are way busier than usual. I let out a long groan and Jett watches me from his booster seat.

"What's wrong, Mommy?"

"Nothing, baby."

The store is packed with parents buying stuff

for their kids. The school supply aisle looks like a tornado ran through it. To make matters worse, I totally forgot the paper the school gave me which had his school supply list on it, so I have to look it up on my phone and then carry my phone in one hand and hold Jett's hand in the other so he doesn't get lost in the crowd of shoppers. That leaves me no hands for putting stuff into our shopping cart.

Things were so much easier when Jett could sit in the shopping cart while I ran errands. Now he's a "big boy" and doesn't like sitting in the "baby cart", which is cute, but not always helpful.

Jett watches in awe as I pick out the required items on the list. Crayons, markers, pencils, paper, scissors, glue sticks, dry erase markers, and boxes of tissues. He likes to toss each item into the cart as we find it, and despite all the people here, that part goes by quickly. Then the hard part starts.

"Okay, now we get to find you a backpack and lunch kit and pencil case!"

We go to the pencil case section first, and there's a huge array of every theme you can think of from princesses to dinosaurs and even something I can only describe as fuzzy robot monsters. Jett looks at each one with precision and care as if choosing the wrong pencil case will somehow ruin his first year of school. After the longest time, he finally turns and looks up at me.

"Where's the dirt bike one?"

"Sweetie, I don't think they have a dirt bike pencil case."

He frowns, his little eyebrows pulling together in a way that makes him look just like his dad. "I want a dirt bike one."

"I'm sorry, they don't have one."

I do a quick search on my phone to see if I can find a dirt bike pencil case, but it's no use. Frowning, Jett looks at them again and finally chooses the fuzzy robot monster case.

He does the same thing with lunch kits. He studies each one, turns some of them around to see the image on the back, and then looks up at me, stumped. "I don't want a lunch kit."

"Do you want to bring your lunch in a paper bag?" I say with a snort.

He shakes his head. "I'll just eat with you like I always do."

My heart hearts. I don't think Jett fully realizes what kindergarten is. I kneel down in the middle of the lunch kit aisle with kids and parents all around and look my son in his eyes. "Sweetie, when you start school, you won't eat lunch with me. You'll eat lunch at the school with your new friends. That's why you need a lunch kit so you can bring your food with you."

His eyes widen. "You won't be at school with me?"

I shake my head and he looks very alarmed at this stunning new revelation. I'm worried he'll start crying, so instead, I divert his attention to the back-packs. Luckily, he zeroes in on a cool backpack that has a BMX bike on it. It's not exactly a dirt bike, but it's close enough. He beams when I tell him he can have it and he wears it around the store for the rest of the trip.

I decide not to go back to the lunch kits any time soon. Maybe I'll just buy him one when he's not with me. With the rest of the school supplies checked off the list, Jett and I swing by the clothing section and get him some new outfits. He's bored by any clothing that isn't an official dirt bike brand, so he lets me choose some shorts, pants, and shirts, without much input.

We're waiting in the check out line when Jace calls me about an hour later.

"Hey, babe," I say when I answer the phone.

"Are you still shopping?" he asks. Music plays in

the background and it sounds like he's probably working out at the gym.

"We're almost done. If you happen to know where I can find a dirt bike themed lunch kit, that would be helpful."

He chuckles. "Maybe we can put a dirt bike patch on a plain one."

"That's a good idea. You're a genius, babe."

"I know, I know," he says playfully. "So anyway, I was calling to see if you got groceries while you were out?"

I bite my lip. How did I forget to get groceries? Our kitchen is basically a barren wasteland with how low we are on food. I've been meaning to go grocery shopping for a week but we're so busy and it's always so easy to buy takeout food instead of cooking. If I hadn't lost track of time earlier, I probably would have remembered to get groceries. That was the plan, after all.

I heave a sigh. "I totally forgot. Ugh, I'm so sorry. I'll turn around and go get some right now."

"Nah, it's okay," Jace says. "How about we get pizza for dinner tonight?"

"Sounds good," I say, but I feel like crap. We need groceries. But now it's late, and the store is so busy, and Jett is starting to get antsy and tired, and getting groceries now would just be a huge pain.

As we move through the checkout line, I can't help but notice another mom at a nearby register. She reminds me of that woman from the school the other day because her hair looks nice too, and she's wearing a nice outfit. Her son looks to be about Jett's age, maybe a little younger. He's wearing khaki shorts and a button up shirt that's tucked in, as well as cute little socks and loafers. But it's the hair that gets my attention. His dark hair is cut into a neat little hair style, parted on the side, and gelled into place. He looks like a sweet little gentleman.

And here I am with my son who is wearing a ratty old T-shirt, has super messy overgrown hair, and looks like he just crawled out of a dirt pit.

Quick, someone give me an award for Mother of the Year.

FOUR

ONE OF MY favorite parts of the day is around nine in the evening, after Jett's gone to bed and the hustle and bustle of busy days finally calms down. Jace and I like to curl up on the couch and catch up on our favorite TV shows. While at the store earlier today, I'd picked up some fall scented candles, and the smell of warm cinnamon apple permeates the living room while I snuggle up to my man, the glow of the television lighting up the room.

My finger runs across my heart necklace while we watch TV. It was a gift from Jace on our anniversary years ago, and it has both his and Jett's fingerprints on either side of the heart pendant. I love it so much.

On the kitchen table in the other room is a pile

of school supplies. Before Jett had to take a bath and go to bed, we had taken the time to write his name with a Sharpie on every single thing, as the school's instructions told us to do. I let him practice writing his own name and it's so cute. I want to get his handwriting printed out onto a sticker or something so I can keep it with me always.

"I can't believe our little baby is growing up," I say, looking up at Jace. His eyes are fixed on the television, and I worry he didn't hear me, but then he smiles.

He peers down at me and places a kiss on my forehead. "Before we know it, he'll be graduating high school."

"No, no, no, I don't want to hear it!" I say playfully. "He is my little baby and that's all he'll ever be."

"Nope, he'll be a teenage chick magnet amateur motocross racer before you know it." Jace clicks his tongue. "He might even outshine me on the track one of these days."

"Ugh. I don't want him to grow up," I whine. I realize I sound a lot like Jett did when he said he didn't want to eat lunch without me. "I don't want him to go to school."

"Aww, it'll be okay," Jace says. His hand slides

down my hair, comforting me while we watch TV. I snuggle closer against his chest, smell the scent of his body wash mixed with the laundry detergent on his shirt. He smells so good I want to snuggle up against him and never leave.

"I feel guilty every time I talk about Jett at work," he says a few moments later.

"What do you mean?"

"Park is nice about it, and I know he loves Jett too, but I always get this underlying sense that he's a little jealous, ya know?" He frowns, like he feels bad about what he just said, then he slides his hand down his leg, a nervous gesture he does sometimes. "I think he and Becca really want their own kid, and here we are rubbing our kid in their faces all the time."

"They do love Jett," I say with a nod. "I don't think that makes Park upset or anything. I think he can love Jett and also wish he had his own kid."

"I still feel bad anytime I talk about Jett around him."

"Well, you shouldn't. Park would do anything for our son. He's basically family to them."

"I suppose you're right," Jace says, squeezing me closer to him.

He goes back to watching the show, but now that he's brought up this topic, my mind starts to go wild with worries and stresses. Becca is my best friend in the whole world and she totally loves Jett! She would never be resentful of him. But just because she loves the kid himself doesn't mean she's not a little bit jealous, right? I know she wants her own kids, and I know they're trying for a baby. Every now and then I expect her to show up to work one day and excitedly tell me that she's pregnant. But it never happens.

I'm sure it will happen soon, though. Then Jett will have a little friend to play with. Who knows? Maybe I'll try to get pregnant the same time she does and then we can raise our kids together. That would be fun not being the only one changing diapers and running on a lack of sleep—of course it might be bad for the Track if its two front office employees are low on sleep for months at a time.

I smile to myself at the image of Becca and me with newborns and tell myself that whatever happens, happens.

Half an hour later, I feel Jace slowly drift off to sleep beside me. His breathing deepens and his arm goes slack around my shoulders. I peek up at him to make sure he's fully out, and then I take the remote and change the show to something girly and silly that he doesn't like. Hey, he can't complain if he's not awake.

Becca texts me a funny meme, and when I finish replying to her, I open up social media just to scroll aimlessly while I'm watching TV. I don't know what inspires me to think about that woman I talked to at school registration day. For some reason I can still remember her social media handle that was printed on her keychain. @LawsonMomLife. It was kind of funny to me because Lawson is such a small town, it's not like we have this bustling mom population or anything. We're just a small town with people who mostly mind their own business.

Out of curiosity, I search her username and find her account.

Holy crap! She's got over half a million followers! Jace is the most famous person in this town and he only has a hundred thousand followers. This woman must be some kind of icon I know nothing about.

A whole hour passes while I'm scrolling through her feed, watching her videos and reading her super long captions. I know there are a lot of online "influencers," but I always thought those were mostly younger women who were skilled in makeup, or hair, or nails, or even fashion. I didn't even realize that there's this entire other world of influencers called "mommy bloggers" who get famous by posting about being a mom.

As I scroll through her page, I'm fascinated, and horrified, and inspired and… guilty? This woman really is a rock star. She has four kids! And they all look just as put together as she is, with adorable outfits, socks that actually match, styled hair, and clean faces.

Her house is gorgeous, too. I can tell by scrolling through her pictures that she lives in the Oakwood subdivision a few miles away. It's a nice neighborhood with new brick homes that are all jammed in close together, but the houses are so nice that no one cares about the small yards. She has a pool in her back yard, one she frequently decorates for dinner parties and for her kids' birthday parties.

She's incredible. She posts recipes and crafts and games that are all stuff you can do for your kids. Her house is stunning on the inside as well as the outside. Her living room is tastefully decorated, the kitchen has a cute farmhouse theme, and even her bathroom has artwork and hand towels that match the shower curtain. Her real life house looks like one of those fancy home magazines. I'm in love.

I also feel really guilty. I look up from my phone and take in the sight of my house. It's also a new build, custom built to our specifications, and only a few years old. It's nice and new just like hers but… it doesn't look like it. Our furniture is a mixture of old stuff from our apartment and new stuff we bought with seemingly no rhyme or reason. I mean seriously, why did we buy a gray couch when our TV stand is brown wood? It looks ugly. It doesn't look anything like Elle, the LawsonMomLife lady's house.

Plus Jett's toys are all over the place. We try to introduce him to all kinds of different toys so he can learn while he's playing, but his favorite toys hands down are dirt bikes. The house is littered with them. The laundry room is basically a dumping ground for all clothes clean and dirty, our bathroom has random towels in all different colors, and our kitchen is kind of a nightmare.

Jace shifts in his sleep, then wakes up slowly. He blinks, realizing he's still on the couch. "Ready for bed?" he asks.

"Am I a bad mom?" I reply.

His face wrinkles up in sleepy confusion. "No. Of course not."

I knew he would say that, because he loves me and he has to say things like that. But after spending two hours on this woman's social media... I'm not so sure I am a good mom. Or a good wife. In fact, I think I suck at it.

FIVE

I BARELY GET any work done at The Track the next day. I had planned on restocking the T-shirts, filling up the vending machines, and making some promotional graphics for our Facebook page, but before I know it, it's lunch time and I've done nothing but sit on the work computer all day.

Becca has been dealing with the gym equipment sales rep for most of the morning. She's better with stuff like that. I get nervous around salesmen and end up agreeing to buy stuff I don't really want, but she'll hold her ground and check out all the options before making the right choice and not spending any more money than she wants to.

When she walks back to the front office with the sales guy, we both tell him bye and watch him walk out. She sits on the stool next to me and blows out a long sigh. "Ugh, that was exhausting."

"Did you get anything good?"

"I got a maintenance plan where they fix all the machines for the next five years for just a hundred bucks."

"Nice."

Becca examines her manicure, which is purple sparkles, then reaches over and straightens the various brochures and business cards on the front desk. "What have you been up to today?"

"Not much," I say, closing off the social media page on the work computer.

I usually browse the app on my phone, but this morning when I got to work, I'd pulled it up and fawned over LawsonMomLife's photos and posts, reading every single caption and feeling both amazed and ashamed. She's an incredible mom. She has this philosophy that her husband should be treated like a king and her children should be treated like royalty.

I know that sounds weird, and kind of sexist, but it's different the way she talks about it. She goes on and on about how her family is her legacy and how her kids and husband are the most important things in her life and she wants to give them the best life possible.

My son and my husband are the most important things to me. I'd be lost without either one of them. I love them more than I can love anyone. So why don't I treat them like royalty? The thought has been burrowing into my mind all day.

And part of having a happy family, according to Elle, is to value your own self worth, too. *Know your worth and then add tax*. It's one of her favorite sayings because she posts about it all the time. She claims that maintaining her hair and nails and always looking nice is what adds to her self esteem, and therefore her self worth. It also makes her look like the woman she wants the world to see her as.

If I dressed nice and looked nice every day, would I have the courage to talk to the sales guys without getting swindled into buying stuff I don't want? Would all of the haters who love Jace and hate me for marrying him suddenly realize that I *am* good enough for him if I *look* good enough for him?

What about Jett? Will he be proud to call me his mom when I show up to school looking like a bombshell badass instead of my frumpy yoga-pants, messy-hair self that I normally am?

These thoughts are plaguing me. I can't stop

scrolling through Elle's profile, wishing my life looked more like hers. (Except for the four kids part… not sure I'm ready for four kids all at once.)

"So what do you think?" Becca says. Her head tilts as she watches me and I suddenly realize she's been talking to me this whole time while I was lost in thoughts of how I'm not good enough to be a mom like Elle.

"Sorry," I say, feeling a blush creep to my cheeks. "I wasn't paying attention. What'd you say?"

"Ouch," she says, putting a hand to her chest.

"Sorry, it's not you," I say with a slight laugh. "I'm just lost in my own world."

A look of concern flashes across her face. "Everything okay?"

"Yep. I probably need more caffeine," I joke.

"Okay, well I was saying that after work we should go shopping because I want to buy Jett some new school clothes."

"Aww, you don't have to do that. He's got new clothes."

"I'm the godmother and I want to!" she protests. "I was at Old Navy the other day and they have such cute clothes for little kids! I want to get him one of everything."

"Well, if you insist," I say, nudging her with my shoulder. "Did you know Jett's mom could use some new clothes too?"

She laughs so hard she snorts. "Too bad I'm not Jett's mom's godmother!"

We make plans to go to the next town over and do some shopping after work today. I had wanted to be home all evening so I can get started on my goal to become just like Elle the LawsonMomLife influencer, but spending some time with my bestie is too fun to pass up.

The last day has been eye-opening for me. I'm seeing life as a wife and mother in an entirely new light… the light of Elle's influencer life. And I want it. I want it badly. I want the beautiful house and the nice outfits and styled hair and picture-perfect life. Why? Because my life is perfect. I have the best husband and the best son and they deserve the absolute best in life.

The way I see it, there are three main parts of my life that need to be spruced up:

My family.

My house.

And me.

Doing it all at once might be too much to handle, so I think I'll try to pick one thing and make

it perfect first. Then I'll move onto the next one.
I'm saving myself for last, because while I want to
look stunning every single day just like Elle does,
I'm not sure I have the energy to figure out hair and
makeup and cute outfits right now. Plus, my family
matters more.

When I remember that my Aunt Truly's new
hair salon is right next to the shopping center near
Old Navy, it's an even better idea to go shopping
after work, because Jett needs to get his unruly mess
of hair trimmed into a neat haircut before he starts
school. Becca drives us in her shiny new SUV.
When she bought the car, she'd said it was so she
would already have the perfect family vehicle for
when she and Park got pregnant. So far, it hasn't
happened, but I'm sure it will soon.

Becca isn't kidding about her Old Navy clothes
obsession. She buys Jett just about every single outfit
they have in his size. I tell her she's going overboard, but she doesn't care. It makes her happy to
spoil my kid, so who am I to complain?

Afterward, we walk down the shopping center
to my Aunt Truly's hair salon. She used to work
near the C&C BMX Park, but now she's on this
part of town in a busier, newer area. Her salon is
sleek and modern. She's happy to see us, even

though I feel a little guilty for not calling ahead for an appointment. Jett rushes up and squeezes her in a hug.

"I can always fit you in," she says, smiling warmly a me when I apologize for the walk-in.

She reaches out and runs her fingers through my long hair. "What would you like done today?"

"Actually, it's not for me," I say, ruffling Jett's head. "It's for him."

"Oooh," she beams. "Just a trim?"

"Nope," I say, helping Jett climb into the salon chair. "Chop it all off. Make it a sleek, professional little boys' haircut."

Both Aunt Truly and Becca's jaws drop.

"Are you sure?" my aunt says.

"Yup."

Jett has only had a few haircuts in his life. He likes his hair long wild and crazy. Actually, I don't think he *likes* it so much as he just doesn't care.

"What do you think?" I ask him. "Should we give you a nice new hair cut so you look good for school?"

He shrugs. "Sure."

SIX

BEFORE I KNOW IT, the last day of summer has passed, and we're waking up on Jett's first day of school. He picked out his first day of school outfit last night after I helped him sort through his old, ratty clothes and realize that his new school clothes would be a better idea for making a good first impression. He chose a pair of khaki shorts, his new Vans shoes, (complete with a fresh, new pair of socks, and a blue and white button up plaid shirt that Becca got him.

He looks like such a perfect little gentleman. I comb over his hair and gel it in place, and then stand back and admire my sweet boy.

"You look so handsome," I say.

He rolls his eyes.

"Whoa, good lookin' dude," Jace says when we walk into the kitchen. He'd normally be at work by now, but we're both taking the morning off so we can take Jett to school. Tomorrow, he'll start riding the school bus. Luckily, he has a few friends who live nearby, so he'll have someone to sit with on the bus.

LawsonMomLife posted a video to her social media about how she prepares her kids' school lunches. She makes sandwiches and cuts out the bread with cute cookie cutters, then slices up fruit and arranges it nicely in plastic cups. She uses healthy veggie chips and all organic foods. I want my son to have a good life but I don't want to torture him with veggie chips, so I made him a lunch that was similar, but it also had some Doritos. I found a cool smiley face cookie cutter that cut his sandwich into a circle and made a little smiley face intention into the bread. I hope he loves it.

I also included a handwritten note. Jett can't read much since he's only five, but I wrote: "I love you" using a heart for the word love, and then signed it "Mom". That part was my idea, since LawsonMomLife didn't post about lunch notes. I think he'll like the surprise.

Jace's parents, Julie and Gary, video call us while

MY TRUST IN YOU

Jace is driving us to the school. I hold out my phone so Jett can see his grandparents.

"Hey guys!" I say, waving into the phone. His parents live in California, so they like to video chat frequently so they can see us. They especially love talking to their grandson.

"I heard it was a very special day today," Gary says.

"Yes, I heard that, too," Julie says, grinning into the camera. "I wonder what happens today…"

"It's my first day of school!" Jett says.

"Are you excited?" Julie asks.

"Yes!" Jett holds up his lunch kit and backpack, showing them off. He hasn't mentioned the lunch thing again, so hopefully he'll be fine when school lunch time rolls around and I'm not with him.

He then shows his grandparents his new shoes and clothes, and they fawn over everything, being the perfect grandparents that they are. Then they talk more to Jace and me, saying they want to come visit soon. We have a guest bedroom that they stay in when they visit, but it occurs to me now that the room is total crap. It's just a bed with a dresser and an old television. The room isn't decorated or anything. I bet LawsonMomLife has a stunning, professionally decorated guest room that makes all her guests feel like movie stars when they stay over. I make a mental note to spruce up our pathetic little guest room into something worthy of Jace's parents.

"So, Mom," Julie says to me. It's so cute how she calls me *Mom* now. "How are you feeling about your little boy going to school?"

"I'm excited for him," I say, tossing Jett a grin.

"Have you cried yet?"

"What? No," I say with a chuckle. "Why would I cry?"

Gary chuckles right back at me. "Oooh, boy. Julie cried her butt off when Jace started school."

"You did?" I say, laughing.

"Oh yes." Julie nods. "I was super emotional."

Beside me, Jace snorts while driving his truck. "I don't really remember my first day of school."

"Well I remember it enough for the both of us. I was a bawling, pitiful, mess. I just couldn't believe my little baby was starting school."

"Mom, you don't have to cry," Jett says from the back seat. He holds out his little hand to me, but he can't quite reach my shoulder from back there.

I lean back and squeeze his hand. "Don't worry, baby. I won't cry."

We end the phone call right as Jace parks at the school. The parking lot is full of parents who had the same idea we did of taking their kid to the first day. Jett holds hands with both of us as we make our way into the office and down the long hallway toward the kindergarten hallway that's to the left. There are four kindergarten classes at Lawson Elementary. Jett has been assigned to Mrs. Roy's class.

"Wow," Jace says as we walk into the classroom. "This place is awesome." He turns to me with wide eyes. "Can I go here too?"

I grin and nudge him with my elbow. "No, you're way too old."

The classroom is very impressive. It's colorful and full of stuff, and yet somehow neat and orderly at the same time. There's a big fluffy rug at the front of the room, tiny little tables and chairs with each kid's name on it, a cubby section for the kids to put their backpacks, and lots of books and learning toys. There's even a reading corner with beanbags and pillows. It looks awesome.

I get that familiar sinking feeling in my stomach as we wait our turn to meet the teacher. All the women in the room are watching my husband. Even the lady who looks like she's twice his age— she's just ogling him like he's a model in a dirty magazine. But he's not a model, he's my freaking husband.

I step a little closer to him. Jett stands in front of us, eagerly waiting to meet his teacher. When it's our turn, Mrs. Roy is a total delight. She's young, probably not quite thirty yet, and full of energy. She hugs Jett and welcomes him to her classroom, then shows us where his chair and cubby are located.

He drops off his backpack and runs to sit in his chair, which is at a table that three other kids share. Across the room, a kid starts crying and screaming, begging her mom not to leave her in class. Mrs. Roy rushes over to help smooth over the situation. My stomach knots. What if Jett starts crying? Does he realize that we will leave him here each day?

"Well, buddy," Jace says, kneeling down so that he's eye-level with our son. "It's about time for me and Mom to go back to work. We will come pick you up after school. Does that sound good?"

My heart skips a beat waiting for Jett's response. I don't want him to cry. I'd feel so awful leaving him here if he's kicking and screaming the whole time. But my son surprises me. He nods eagerly at his dad.

"Bye, Dad," he says, waving at him. He turns to me. "Bye, Mommy."

Jace and I exchange surprised looks. This is going much better for us than for a few other kids in the classroom. We hug him goodbye, and I walk slowly to the door, nervously expecting my son to rush after me and beg me to stay.

But he doesn't.

As we walk down the hallway, I turn back and peer into the classroom door. Jett is excitedly talking to the little boy sitting next to him. He's perfectly fine.

"Well, that was easy," Jace says, wrapping an arm around my waist.

"Super easy."

We reach the doorway to the parking lot and Jace pushes it open, letting me go first. "How about before we go back to work, we stop at a diner and get some breakfast to celebrate our amazing accomplishment of raising a good kid?"

"Sounds good," I say, peering up at my handsome husband.

He grins back at me. And then I burst into tears.

I don't even know why. My chest swells and my heart clenches and my little boy is back in that building without me, and he's okay. Everything is okay. He's growing up and he's becoming a little person of his own. And I have absolutely no idea why I'm crying, but Jace's mom was right. I am a total mess.

"Aww, baby," my husband says as he opens the truck door for me. "I love you."

I smile and brush away the tears from my cheek. "I love you, too."

SEVEN

LUCKILY, my tears don't last too long. After a lovely breakfast with Jace at our favorite local diner, I've got other things on my mind. While eating a huge breakfast plate, my hard-working husband had made a little comment. It was an innocent comment, and it totally didn't mean anything, but my brain has latched onto it and won't let it go.

He had just taken a huge bite of hash browns and said, "These are so good. Diner food is so good. You can't make 'em like this at home."

And I know he didn't say the word "you" in a way that meant ME, specifically. He just meant you in general. Especially since I've never tried to make hash browns, and Jace has tried a couple of times… if anything, he was referring to himself when he said that comment. But the fact remains that Jace loves hash browns and he thinks they can only be delicious when you get them at a diner.

I want to prove him wrong. Not just with the hash browns, but with all meals. I want to start cooking in my house. Real food. Not just easy food like the spaghetti that I usually make.

At work, I'm looking up recipes on the work computer and watching cooking videos, trying to figure out which delicious meal I'm capable of making for my family tonight. It's Jett's first day of school, after all, and I think it'd be fun if the family can sit around the table and eat a good meal to celebrate this new milestone in our son's life.

Suddenly, Becca smacks into the front counter, having run up here from the back hallway, I guess. I didn't hear her coming. I didn't even see her coming until she's suddenly next to me, grabbing the work phone.

"The Track, this is Becca," she says, giving me a weird look from the corner of her eye. "How can I help you today?"

I go back to my cooking videos. When she's finished with her call, I get the weird feeling that she's looking at me. I turn to her. She *is* looking at me. Her hands stiffly resting on her hips.

"What?" I say.

"Earth to Bayleigh," she says, waving her hands in front of my face. "Are you a real human or some kind of robot?"

I make a face. "What are you talking about?"

"The phone rang three different times!" She stares at me like that's supposed to mean something.

"It did?"

"Yes, and I yelled for you to get it, and it kept ringing, so I thought maybe you left the front office without telling me and I had to drop everything and come answer the phone."

"Whoa," I say, glancing at the computer screen. Have I been that involved in my own little world of looking up cooking lessons that I didn't even notice the phone ringing? "Sorry. I guess I was distracted."

"Everything okay?" Becca asks, her annoyed expression turning softer.

"Yeah. I just want to start cooking dinner for my family."

My best friend snorts out a laugh. "*You* want to start cooking?"

"It's not a crazy idea," I say, rolling my eyes.

"No... but... you're not a good cook."

"Well, I want to become a good cook. Jace deserves a wife who can cook."

"Jace already has an amazing wife, you dork." She playfully punches me on the shoulder.

"I still want to make something good for dinner tonight. Something to celebrate Jett's first day of school."

She peers at the computer screen. "So what are you thinking of making?" Her eyes widen when she sees the video on the screen. "Lasagna?"

I shrug. "I love lasagna."

"Yeah, but it's kind of hard to make."

"It doesn't seem that hard. You just layer the ingredients and then bake it. Easy."

"I could come over and help you," she says.

I shake my head. "No, thanks. That's really nice of you to offer but I want to do it myself just to prove that I can.

She quirks an eyebrow. I can't tell if she's proud of me for wanting to try, or scared because it's such a bad idea. "The last thing he needs is you burning the house down trying to do something you're inherently terrible at."

This time I snort out a laugh. I guess it's not the proud thing, but scared one. "I'm not that bad of a cook."

Luckily, a customer walks in the door at this very moment and ends our conversation, which is a good thing because I'm not sure I'd win that argument. I've never been good at cooking. It seems like cooking is some natural-born skill that everyone else has except for me. But a perfect mom like Lawson-MomLife cooks meals in her house. And I'm going to do it too.

I LET Jace take off work a little early to go pick up our son without me. I wanted to be there, but I also want to run to the grocery store to get everything on my list to make the perfect "simple" lasagna, according to the recipe. But with each ingredient I add to the shopping card, my nerves get a little more anxious. It's supposed to be simple, but there's so many things to do. I also found a garlic bread recipe that uses three types of cheese, real garlic cloves, mayo, and butter. I toss it all into my cart even though I'm pretty sure we have plenty of butter at home. I just don't want to mess this up.

When I pull into the driveway, Jace and Jett are tossing a frisbee in the front yard.

"How'd the first day of school go?" I ask, bending down to be eye-level with Jett as he runs up to me.

"It was so fun!" he says right before he tumbles into a long ramble about all the things he loves about school. My heart bursts with joy.

Jace loads up all the grocery bags on one arm and carries them inside, and when he walks back outside, he kisses me hello.

"What's with the weird groceries?" he asks.

"What do you mean?" Suddenly I'm afraid he's going to say he hates lasagna.

"It's just not the normal stuff we usually get."

"That's because I have a special surprise for tonight." I bat my eyelashes a bit as I pick up Jett, who has been reaching up for me to hold him. He's five now, and probably too old to be held, but I love snuggling my little boy even if it's a struggle to carry him inside.

Jace doesn't seem too worried about my idea to cook dinner. In fact, he nods, and offers to give Jett his bath so I don't have to worry about it.

Once I'm alone in the kitchen, I pull up the lasagna tutorial video on my phone and get to work. After Jett's bath time, he and Jace play in the living room. Jace tries to come in and see if I need any help, but I shush him and tell him to go away. The perfect wife doesn't need help, so neither do I.

An hour later, my lasagna looks amazing. I

followed all the instructions perfectly, pausing my tutorial video and making sure I did the exact same things. I lean against the kitchen island, biting my lip in anticipation. Maybe being an awesome wife and mom isn't as hard as I worried.

Then I smell burning.

"Crap," I hiss, rushing to the top oven where I'd put the cheesy garlic bread. I completely forgot to set a time for it! It only needed twenty minutes and it's been closer to thirty-five. Grabbing my oven mitts, I pull out the mostly-burnt bread and hold back tears. My lasagna looks good but the bread is ruined.

"Smells good," Jace says a few minutes later.

"It's not good. It's terrible."

He appraises the kitchen table, which I've decorated with plates and napkins and a pitcher of sweet tea. Then he looks at the lasagna and bread which is on the counter, ready to be served. "Looks amazing to me."

"The bread is burned."

"Nah," he says, cutting off a piece and taking a bite. "It's still good."

I frown. "You can't possibly mean that."

"Of course I mean it." He calls for Jett to come take a seat at the table, and then Jace makes all of us a plate, complete with salad I had forgotten I set out earlier.

"This is beautiful," Jace says, smiling at me over a bite of lasagna. "Jett, what do we tell Mommy for making us this amazing dinner?"

"Thank you, Mommy," Jett says. His face has marinara sauce on it when he grins at me.

"You don't think it's totally gross?"

Both of my boys shake their heads at me, their mouths too full of the meal I cooked to say anything in reply.

EIGHT

IT ISN'T until my head hits the pillow that I realize how tired I am. It's been a long day, with the excitement of Jett's first day of school, the dinner-cooking fiasco, and me spending way more time than I care to admit looking up stuff online that will help me be the perfect wife and mom. Jace and I have a television in our master bedroom—something some people tell me is a bad idea, but I don't care. I've heard it's bad for your sleep schedule to have a TV in the room. But there's nothing I love more than crawling into bed after a nice shower and watching my favorite shows for a bit before going to sleep. I always either set the sleep timer on the TV, or Jace turns it off after I've fallen asleep.

He's in the shower right now, so I'm watching a girly show I know he doesn't care for, but I'm not paying much attention. I'm thinking of my plans. When he emerges from the bathroom wearing only a towel, I can't help but check him out. He's gorgeous from head to toe, with tanned skin, toned muscles, and that sexy smirk of his.

"Hey, beautiful," he says, sauntering into the room with that towel barely hanging onto his hips.

"How do you look so sexy all the time?" I muse.

He grins. "I could ask you the same thing."

I hold my arms up and he lowers himself onto the bed, his body warm against mine. His arms wrap underneath me and I tangle myself in his embrace. He kisses my forehead and then my cheek and neck. I giggle at the tickle of his stubble on my skin, then gasp as he shifts to the side and pulls me on top of him. His strong arms make sure I don't fall. That poor towel never had a chance, and now it's on the floor.

Kissing Jace is like breathing. I need it. I crave it. I tangle my hands in his hair and kiss him like my life depends on it.

It's magic how he undresses me. First he distracts me with making out, and I'm enthralled in the feel of him, the smell of him, the way my body reacts to him. Then the next thing I know my over-sized T-shirt joins the towel on the floor.

Making love with Jace is better than breathing. He is slow and loving and magical. He makes me feel like no one could ever be loved more than he loves me. As the months and years go on in our relationship, the lovemaking only gets better. I can't imagine spending one single day of my life without this man.

Later, when we're dressed again, snuggling in bed watching TV, I trace my finger over the ab indentions on his chest, barely paying attention to the show. Sometimes I just sit here and think: *I am Jace's wife. Holy crap, I'm Jace's wife!*

But sometimes I don't feel like a wife. I just feel like I always feel… the way I've felt ever since Jace and I started dating. It's not a bad feeling because I'm in love and I'm happy, but I guess I thought being married would suddenly feel completely different. Like maturity and adulthood. Like success. Like we've got everything all figured out. But all that getting married really did was change my last name.

Sure, we're still in love and happy, but I still feel

like a kid. I don't feel like someone who should even be allowed to be married and raise a kid, when I feel so immature myself. Maybe this is why I've become obsessed with Elle from LawsonMom-Life... maybe it's all my insecurities of not being good enough finally rising up and telling me it's time to grow up and mature.

"Babe?" I say, flattening my hand on his chest and looking up at him.

"Hmm?" he murmurs, glancing down at me.

"Do you think I'd be able to take off work next week?"

His brow lifts. "Why?"

"I have a lot of things I need to do, things I've been putting off. I'd like to unpack the rest of our boxes and get our house organized and decorated. And I keep thinking I'll never get anything done if I don't take some time alone to do it. And with Jett in school now, it's the perfect time."

He considers it for a moment. "I could take off work and help you. But I'll have to check my client schedule and see when I can get a week off."

"No, I don't want help. This is something I want to do on my own."

"Are you sure? It sounds boring."

I grin. "I don't think it'll be boring… I think it'll be fun. Plus…" I bite my lip. Jace and I are both self-employed at the same business we co-own with our best friends. So deep down I know that there is no *my* money or *his* money. It's just our money. Maybe that's why it feels so awkward for me to spend it on stuff I want. Or maybe it's because, deep down, I know the only reason I have this job is because of Jace's expertise with dirt bikes. It's not like I could have started the business on my own, so I have him to thank for our savings account.

Jace slides my hair out of my face, his fingers lingering on my cheek. "What is it, babe?"

I take a deep breath, but then I'm right back to biting my lip again. "It sounds kind of stupid, but… I want to decorate the house."

"So decorate the house." He says it so matter-of-factly, like it's not a big deal at all, when it really is.

"No… I mean… I want to throw out some old stuff I don't like and then buy new stuff."

He nods, brows lifting a bit as if he agrees with me. "Sounds good."

"Really?"

"Of course."

I sit up on my elbow a bit so I can look at him. "So I can buy some new furniture, and bookshelves, and like, decoration items? Wall art and stuff?"

"Baby, it's your house, too. You can put whatever you want in it."

"So if I painted the walls pink and hung a disco ball in every single room, you'd be okay with that?"

His nose crinkles up. "No way. That would be so ugly. But I know you, and you wouldn't fill the house with disco balls. Whatever decorations you want are fine with me."

"Really? You're just giving me free rein to re-do the house?"

"Yep. And it should be fine if you take off work. Will Becca be helping you?"

I shake my head. "No, she'll keep working. I already kinda talked to her about it and she was fine with it."

"You know my client, Jack? His mom keeps asking if we're hiring or have any part time jobs because she's bored being a stay-at-home-mom. Maybe we could ask her to fill in at The Track for a week, help Becca out and all that?"

"That would be perfect. Then I can take a week to myself and not feel guilty about it."

Jace leans over and kisses me. "Then consider it done."

"Babe?" I say a moment later when he's gone back to watching TV. "We should discuss the budget. Like, how much money should I spend on this project?"

"Just whatever you feel is needed," he says without giving it a single thought. And yeah, I love that my husband just lets me do anything, but I also want his input on this.

"I think we should let a spending limit," I say. "I don't want to go overboard, but I don't want to cheap out, either." Pictures of LawsonMomLife's amazing home fill my thoughts. I want a home like hers. What could that possibly cost?

"Okay… so, five grand? Ten?"

My jaw drops. "Ten thousand dollars? No way. Not that much."

"So, five?" He shrugs. "That works for me."

I consider it, realizing I have no idea what a house full of nice décor could cost. "Maybe three to five… or six… but not ten."

Jace laughs, shaking his head slightly at me. "I love you, Babe. You might be worrying too much… just do what makes you happy and as long as we have the money in the bank, go for it. I trust you."

I breathe a soft little sigh, gazing up at Jace's eyes. He has so much faith and trust in me, and yet I have no idea what I'm doing. He deserves the best wife on the planet.

So that's what I'll become.

NINE

IT'S incredible what I can get done when my kid is at school, I don't have to go to work, and I have a ton of energy thanks to several cups of coffee. It's only my second day of taking off work and I've managed to empty every single moving box that was still sitting around the house. Some of the stuff needs to be in boxes for storage because it's just old stuff from my childhood or Jace's previous motocross career. Sentimental stuff we don't want to throw out, but it doesn't really have a place in our house. So instead of leaving this stuff in cardboard boxes that look ugly and misshapen from being tossed around moving trucks, I put all the stuff in plastic tubs and labeled the outside with neatly printed labels. Now the plastic tubs are in the attic, stored away safely and no longer an eyesore.

Cleaning and organizing the stuff we already own was my first task. I even went through all the cabinets and drawers in the kitchen and organized everything we own. We got tons of kitchen items as wedding presents, and I haven't even touched some of it because I don't cook. But that's all about to change.

I found an incredibly easy recipe online for a Mexican-inspired slow cooker chicken soup. This inspired me to open up the brand new slow cooker we got as a wedding gift and get to work. I load it up with chicken, black beans, corn, salsa, chicken broth, seasonings, and cream cheese, then set a timer on my phone for four hours. I timed it so that dinner will be ready right around the time Jace gets off work.

Jett comes home from school about an hour earlier, but I'm prepared for that. Thanks to LawsonMomLife's social media posts, I have a ton of cute kid-friendly snack ideas. Today I think I'll make him apple slices with peanut butter and little chocolate chips on top. The old me would have given him a banana or a bag of graham crackers when he wanted a snack. The new me makes lovingly decorated healthy snacks.

Now I'm loading up Jace's truck with all the things I decided to donate as I clear out our house and prepare to start decorating it. I have online wish lists filled with home décor items that will fit the aesthetic I chose for our house. I'm doing a slight "farmhouse" style but with a modern twist. We don't live on a farm, but we do live on a huge plot of land with a dirt bike track on it, so a more country theme kind of fits our lifestyle.

And it's not just wish lists… I also have a dining room full of stuff I recently purchased. I can't wait to start unpacking it all and setting it around the house. As I load up the last box of donation items into the bed of Jace's truck, I head back inside to grab my purse and keys. The scent of the slow cooker soup is already starting to permeate the kitchen, and it smells amazing. I grin to myself as I walk outside. I feel like everything is really starting to come together. I'm giving Jett an amazing childhood by making him cute and healthy meals, dressing him nicely, and fixing his hair each day. I'm spoiling my husband by learning how to cook and keeping the house clean. I'm spoiling myself by making our house look incredible.

Soon, I'll figure out how to find enough time in the mornings to do my hair and makeup each day. Right now, I'm wearing athleisure clothing—spandex leggings and a tank top because the August weather is so impossibly hot, and a pair of hot pink running shoes that I literally never run in. My hair is in a messy bun on top of my head, but I don't feel guilty for looking like this because I've been working hard all day moving boxes and stuff. Maybe tomorrow I will start dressing nicer.

As I drive past The Track on my way into town, I realize I can't even remember the last day I took off work. Owning a business takes a lot of work, but it's work I enjoy doing. Of course, now that I'm free from the obligations of greeting customers, answering phones, and keeping the place running for a week, it feels good. Maybe I should take time off more often. And once I return next week, I should tell Becca to take a mini vacation as well. She works just as hard as I do.

After dropping off the donations, I decide to swing by a local restaurant. They're famous for their baked goods, but they also have the most amazing sandwiches on super delicious homemade bread. I park Jace's massive truck at the back of the lot so it's easier, and then head inside the restaurant, only to get stuck behind a line of people. I guess a ton of people had the same idea I had. Oh well, I have no where I need to be right now. I can wait for a delicious sandwich.

"Well, hello there!"

I turn around and feel a blush creeping to my cheeks when I realize who just stepped into line behind me. It's Elle. LawsonMomLife herself, right here in line behind me once again. Her brown hair is twisted into a half-up half-down hairstyle that looks casual but probably took forever to style.

"You're the girl I mistook for a nanny," she says, putting a hand to her chest. "I am still so embarrassed about that."

"It's no big deal," I say, smiling a little too big. Why am I suddenly so nervous? Probably because I've been basically stalking this woman online for two weeks. But I'm not a real stalker… I just really like her content and have resonated with her lifestyle. Part of me wants to tell her what a huge inspiration she's been for me, but the other part of me knows I should keep my mouth shut. I'll only sound like a starstruck weirdo if I say anything.

"So how's your little one handling kindergarten?" she asks.

"He loves it."

"That's great! Two of mine loved school and two hated it. Unfortunately my littlest is not a fan right now. He'd much rather be home watching cartoons."

I try to think of something to say, but I have zero experience with having more than one kid and I worry that anything I say to this woman who is practically my hero at the moment would just make me look dumb. I smile.

Elle glances behind me. "Are you here alone?"

"Yeah, just grabbing some lunch."

"Me too. You want to eat together?"

The LawsonMomLife is asking ME to eat lunch with her? I tell her yes, and I try to be cool about it.

We chat about kindergarten and her search for a part time nanny as we wait in line, and once we get our food, we settle into a table in the corner of the restaurant. Elle is beautiful and all put together like some kind of movie star, but as I'm sitting here chatting with her, I realize she's also a nice person. She doesn't act like someone who has a ton of followers online, nor does she act like she's better than anyone else. I keep expecting her to brag about her online fame—I mean, I think I would brag if I was as famous as her—but she doesn't. She's polite to the waiter who refills our drinks and she's always smiling. I think she's inspiring me even more here in person.

"You've got nothing to worry about," she tells me after I express my fears over making sure Jett is raised to be a good person. She takes a sip of her sweet tea then says, "I can tell you're a good mama and you care about your son. That's all it takes."

"Thanks. I'm trying really hard. I don't even know if I want more kids because that seems like such a huge responsibility. It's so hard just keeping up with my one kid!"

She chuckles. "It's harder but also easier in some ways. I already have to make lunches and do bath times. Now I just do it four times. And as soon as the kids get older, they start taking care of themselves so your work load gets a little easier." She grins at me. "Plus, you can start assigning chores and then the kids do some of the housework for you."

"That's a good idea," I say, as if I've heard this advice for the first time. Truth is, I've already read about her advice for how to assign age-appropriate chores for your kids in a way that will teach them to become responsible adults.

"Let's be friends, Bayleigh," she says, pulling out

her phone from her designer handbag. "What's your number?"

My heart leaps into my chest. *Elle wants to be friends with me!*

I give her my number and then she texts me so that I have hers.

I'm so excited it's hard to finish my lunch. I just want to jump up and scream for joy because Elle, the LawsonMomLife influencer, wants to be friends with me. We're having lunch together. This is so freaking cool.

"You know what would be fun?" Elle says as we're walking out to our cars after lunch.

"What's that?"

She looks at me appraisingly, and I guess I pass her appraisal because she says, "You should join the Lawson Elementary PTA."

TEN

I'M SO excited about the idea of joining the PTA. The Parent-Teacher Association is a small group of parents who help out at the school. They throw parties, plan teacher appreciation gifts, and according to Elle, they're an elite group of Lawson moms. I want to be an elite Lawson mom, so I need to be in the PTA. The thing is, you can't just sign up. You have to request to join and then go to a trial meeting of sorts where the PTA board members decide if they want to approve you or not. Elle says she'll make sure I get accepted, but I'm still nervous about it. After all, so many people see me as some kid myself, not as a mature parent.

I stop at The Track on my way back home, eager to tell Jace about this new opportunity, but he's booked up with training clients for the rest of the day. I don't want to interrupt him when he's with a client, so I go home and get to work on unpacking my new decorations.

I decide to start with the living room. I add a new rug that's machine washable so I can clean it when it inevitably gets dirty, some cute artwork on the wall next to the TV, and two modern end tables on either side of the couch. It takes me over an hour to assemble them, but they look so good when I'm done. Plus they have outlets that plug into the wall and then you can charge your phone or plug something into the TV stand. It's so cool and looks great.

I also bought a matching set of picture frames that are fairly big, and I have plans to put black and white family photos in the frames and hang them behind the couch. I don't have the pictures yet, because I need to get them professionally printed, but I do take the time to borrow some of Jace's tools and go through the arduous process of hanging all four frames perfectly level and perfectly spaced apart on the wall. The old Bayleigh would have just hung them up wherever, not measuring or making it perfect, but the new me wants perfection.

It's exhausting work, but the picture frames look great.

I'm feeling pretty pumped about the changes to my house in just two days. All the clutter is gone, things are clean, and some new décor is already sprucing up the place. Plus my house smell delicious and I can't wait to serve this new meal to my family for dinner. But even more than that, I can't wait to tell Jace about the PTA.

I actually got sweaty doing all this decorating and picture-hanging around the house, so I take a quick shower and then stare at myself in the bathroom mirror. After washing my hair these days, I usually just toss it into a messy bun and be done with it. But I've taken all these great steps to improve every other aspect of my life… maybe it's time to start improving myself, too.

I have half an hour until Jett gets off the school bus, so I decide to use the time to actually blow dry my hair and brush it out. I hadn't realized just how long my hair has gotten, but it's well past my shoulders now. I pluck my unruly eyebrows and then dab on some makeup just for fun. Instead of putting on yet another pair of leggings and a tank top, I decide to wear denim shorts and a summery purple shirt my mom gave me. My toenail polish is chipped, so I paint them quickly as I hear the school bus rumbling down the road.

I meet Jett in the driveway. His hair is a little disheveled, probably from recess, but he still looks cute as a button.

"Hey, kiddo," I say, waving to the bus driver as she drives away. "How was school?"

"It was good," he says, hitching his backpack up on his shoulders.

I reach out and ruffle his hair.

"Ouch!" He jerks away, rubbing his forehead. Underneath his hair is a massive bruise and a swollen bump. My heart races.

"What happened?" I stop walking and kneel down, lightly pushing back his hair to see the damage.

"Nothing," he says with a shrug.

I give him a look. "You have a massive bruise and it's all swollen! Did someone hit you?"

Jett's face crinkles up like I just said the most hilarious thing. "No, Mommy."

"Then tell me what happened to your head."

He shrugs again. "I dunno. I just hit it on the playground I guess."

I look him in the eyes. "Are you lying to me?"

I'm already picturing how badly I'm going to

yell if some other person's kid hurt my kid, but Jett just shakes his head. "No, I just fell off the playground and it's fine. It doesn't hurt much."

I stand up. I believe him, but I'm still upset. "Let's go show Daddy and see what he thinks."

We walk over to The Track. I don't like bothering Jace at work, but this is different. This is about our son. I find Jace standing near the bleachers, watching a client ride on the track. He jogs over when he sees us. "What's going on?"

I show him Jett's bruise and Jace's face flashes in concern. Then Jett tells him the same story about falling off the playground.

"Does your head hurt?" Jace asks.

Our son shakes his head.

"Well, let's get some ice on it, and you'll probably feel all better in the morning."

"You don't think it's that big of a deal?" I ask him as he leads us into the main office building to get some ice.

"Nah." He slings an arm around my shoulders. "It's just a little bump. He'll be fine."

I breathe a sigh of relief. Jace has had a million injuries on a dirt bike and he's practically our own private EMT with how much knowledge he has. If he doesn't think it's a big deal, then I won't worry too much.

Jett and I hang out at work for the next hour until Jace gets done with his last client of the day. My apple snack can wait until tomorrow, because Becca has a veggie tray in the break room that Jett snacks on instead. I'm dying to tell Becca about the PTA thing, but I want to tell Jace first so I'm stuck waiting an agonizingly long hour until we walk home as a family. We always enter in the back door instead of the front, so while my husband and son gush over the smell of dinner that's cooking in the slow cooker, they aren't able to notice all the changes I made to the decor today.

"We'll eat dinner in a minute," I say, flourishing my hands toward the living room. "But first, let's see the new living room."

I show them, and they both look less than impressed.

"Cool," Jace says with a head nod. "Looks good."

"It's not *cool*," I say, hands on my hips. "It's *amazing*."

He grins. "Yeah, that's what I meant."

I roll my eyes. "What do you think, Jett?"

He shrugs. "I don't care about the new living room, Mommy. I'm hungry."

I roll my eyes again. They might not appreciate our beautiful living room, but at least it makes me happy. Their moods totally change, however, when I serve them dinner. Mexican-inspired chicken soup only requires tortilla chips on the side, not garlic bread, so there's literally nothing I could have messed up. My family gobbles it down and quickly asks for a second bowl.

I'm beaming with pride as I sit at the table and watch them devour the dinner. I can call this day a success. Jett talks all evening about school, and his new friends, and how much he can't wait until this weekend so he can go ride his dirt bike. I hold back on talking about the PTA until Jace and I are alone in our bed after our son goes to sleep.

I sit cross-legged on the bed and bounce up and down in excitement. "Okay," I say, grinning. "I have really cool news."

Jace perks up and sits next to me. "Let's hear it."

"I met another mom today and she asked me to join the PTA."

"Oh, that's cool," Jace says. "Isn't that the mom thing where you plan parties?"

"It's any parent, not just moms, but yeah."

"And I take it you want to do it?" he asks.

I nod. "They have to approve me first. I'm scared they won't."

He scoffs and leans forward, placing a soft kiss on my forehead. "They'll accept you, babe. And if they won't, they'll have to answer to me."

ELEVEN

MY CLOSET IS BETRAYING ME. The PTA meeting starts in an hour and I have nothing to wear. I've been standing here in the massive closet for longer than I care to admit, looking at all of my clothes and wondering why they all suck. What are you supposed to wear to a PTA meeting? Surely it's classier than what you'd wear for a regular day of shopping at Target or something.

Elle had texted me earlier letting me know how the PTA meetings go when someone is applying for membership. I have to fill out a form, introduce myself, and then attend a regular meeting. Then, after the meeting, they'll decide if they want to offer me full membership. Luckily that part happens after

I've gone, so I won't be getting judged right to my face. But I'll still be getting judged, which isn't exactly a fun idea. Still, being a part of the PTA will be a huge step in the right direction in my goal of becoming an amazing mom.

I need to win these parents over. I need a good outfit. I look up Elle's social media and scroll through her posts, trying to remember if she's posted anything about the PTA before. If she's posted a meeting, that would be even better, then I could see what everyone wears. Unfortunately, there is nothing of the sort on her page. Guess I have to wing it.

Since it's fall, the whole "pumpkin spice" aesthetic is super popular on Elle's social media right now. So I go with that theme and choose a pair of black skinny jeans, knee-high leather boots, a dark green sweater, and a long trendy topaz necklace. It's not yet cold outside, but I fit the fall theme really well. I brush my hair into a low ponytail and put on some makeup. I look way more dressed up than usual, but is it enough for a PTA meeting?

I am all nerves as I drive up to the school's side entrance. Elle told me the meetings are held in the cafeteria and they leave a side door unlocked for us.

There are about ten other cars clumped together in this part of the parking lot, so I've found the right place. I take a deep breath and step out of my car. I hope these people like me. I hope I like them. I want to be a part of this.

The school cafeteria is empty except for two tables in the middle of the room. A third table next to it is filled with cookies, coffee carafes, and other snack foods. About a dozen woman are here, some sitting and chatting, and others standing. I know I told Jace that the PTA means any parent, but I guess only moms care about this sort of thing. I do a quick inventory of their outfits as I walk across the cafeteria. Almost everyone is dressed the same way I am. *Score one for Bayleigh!*

Elle is easy to spot in the crowd because of her big hair and contagious, cheerful laugh. I walk right up to her, so nervous I might pass out.

"Bayleigh!" she says, holding out her arms. I give her a quick hug and she turns to the crowd. "Ladies, this is the new girl I told you about. She's joining us for a try-out meeting today."

I hope my makeup is thick enough to cover the blush that creeps to my cheeks as all eyes turn to me. Most of the women here appear to be in their thirties and forties. Absolutely no one looks like they're in their twenties. I feel like I'm someone's daughter and not a peer.

A quick glance around tells me that many of these women must feel the same way. They offer me polite hellos but most of them don't seem impressed. A couple even scowl in my direction. I swallow.

Soon, the meeting starts, and Elle calls it to session. I realize quickly that she's the PTA president. She sits at the end of the table with a clipboard and a laptop, shoulders back and face poised as a position of authority. I'm not sure if there's assigned seating at a thing like this, but I take the chair next to Elle and no one seems to mind.

"New business," Elle says, flashing a smile to me. "We have a prospective new member. Bayleigh, would you like to introduce yourself to the group?"

"Absolutely," I say, even though I feel the exact opposite. Once again, everyone is looking at me. Should I stand up? No... I don't think so?

I take a deep breath. "My name is Bayleigh Adams. I'm a mom to Jett, who just started kindergarten here, so I'd like to be a member for several years." I'd rehearsed that part on the drive over here, because if I say I'm committed to the

PTA for many years, maybe they'll want me to join. No one seems to care, however. And they also keep looking at me like they expect me to say more.

I smile. "I love helping out, I'm a team player, and I'm someone you can count on to get stuff done. I'd love to be a member here."

"And you're a stay-at-home mom?" a woman to my right asks. She's older, probably late forties, with dark black hair that's cut in a severely sharp bob style. Her makeup is heavy-handed, and her dark rouge lips flatten as she stares at me.

I'm not sure any answer would appease her, but when I say, "No, I work full time," she actually seems slightly impressed.

"Do you work a time-consuming job?" another woman asks. "This association meets bi-monthly from six to eight and it is important to attend every meeting and every monthly fundraiser."

"No, I have plenty of time for the PTA," I say, glancing over at Elle who is smiling politely at me. I hope my anxiety isn't written all over my face. "I work at a business I own, so I'm free to come and go as I need."

"What business is that?" she asks.

"Um, The Track? It's a dirt bike facility."

This gets their attention. "*You* own that massive facility?" the bob haircut woman says.

I nod. "I am co-owner with my husband and two others."

"No way!" Elle says, grabbing my arm. "I didn't know that! That is so cool!"

Her informal enthusiasm is a nice break in the otherwise serious room. She turns to the rest of the group. "She's talking about that big dirt bike facility on the edge of town."

When she turns back to me, there's something new in her eyes. Respect? Happiness?

"You're like totally famous," she says, smiling at me.

"What?" I scoff. "Nah."

"Her husband is the famous one," another woman says. "Jace Adams, right? My son is obsessed with him."

The next several minutes are spent talking about my husband and my business and all about the world of motocross. Everyone seems to think it's really cool that I co-own one of the most popular businesses in town. Even Elle looks at me differently now. Before, she was friendly, but almost in this "big sister" mentor type of way. Now she seems to be looking at me like *she's* the starstruck one, instead of the other way around.

Once the meeting gets back on track, I settle into my seat with a cup of coffee and some sugar cookies. I pay close attention to everything, but don't really have much to say. They go over their various fundraiser activities, and talk about their plans for making Christmas gift baskets for all of the teachers.

Then Elle heaves a sigh and looks out at the small group of people. "Okay, I know we're dreading this part, but it's time to talk about the annual fall banquet…Ashley was supposed to be in charge of it, but as you all know, she broke her back and can't help out at all."

A few people groan. Another woman says, "We should just cancel it. We can't do this without Ashley."

"What's the banquet?" I ask. It's the first time I've spoken since I introduced myself.

"It's our biggest fundraiser of the year," Elle says. "We rent out a facility, cater a nice dinner, have a silent auction and some entertainment and we raise a crap-ton of money. And now we have no one to organize it."

"We'll be completely broke without this event," someone says.

Elle nods. "I don't know what we're going to do."

I bite my lip. Then I say something completely unexpected.

"I'll do it."

TWELVE

THE DECISION WAS UNANIMOUS. Everyone voted to allow me to join the PTA. Of course, that's probably because I volunteered to organize an entire fundraiser banquet—the biggest fundraiser of the entire year—despite not knowing a single thing about organizing a fundraiser banquet.

But I won't let anything stop me from planning the best damn fundraiser banquet this PTA has ever seen.

Plus Elle is kind of my friend now. It's not like we're spending the day texting or hanging out, but she invited me to the PTA and vouched for me, and my dream of living a life just like hers is slowly coming true. I'm so giddy I can't stand it. I even wake up early and cook scrambled eggs, bacon, and toast for Jace and Jett this morning. I think my eggs might be a tad overcooked, but the boys don't care. They both scarf it down like it's the best thing they've ever eaten.

Jace and I wait in the driveway while the school bus picks up Jett. There might be a day when he doesn't want to hug his mom and dad before going to school, but today isn't that day. After he's on the bus, I walk with Jace next door to work. I'm still technically on my vacation, but my house is as good as it can be until all the new décor I ordered arrives in the mail. Today, I think I'll start planning the banquet while hanging out at work.

Jace holds the office door open for me but he doesn't step inside. Instead he leans down and kisses me, lingering on the kiss just a few seconds. I breathe in the fresh scent of his body wash and taste the slight hint of coffee on his breath. It's a good taste. And now I want coffee.

"Love you," he says.

"Love you more." I grin as I step into the office.

"Psh, yeah right," he says playfully, letting the door close behind me.

"Y'all are so freaking cute," Becca says. She's standing near the coffee cart, making herself a cup of "extra cream, slight coffee" as I like to call it.

"You and Park are just as gross," I tease, walking over and pouring myself a cup of coffee.

"I said cute, not gross."

I laugh. "Yeah, but you meant gross."

She chuckles. "Nah. I love watching people suck face in public."

I hip-check her then walk over to the front counter and sit on a barstool.

"Aren't you off this week?" Becca says, sitting next to me. She powers on the work computer. "Jack's mom Misty has been doing a great job filling in for you. She'll be here soon. Should I call her and say she's not needed?"

I shake my head and open up the magical binder in front of me. "I'm not working today, I just wanted to come show you this."

"What exactly is it?" Becca asks, curiously peering at the ugly thing. It's only one-inch wide, but it's covered in Lawson Elementary stickers and has lots of other scrapbook type stickers all over the place.

"This is the banquet-planning binder that the previous PTA member made to help her plan the fundraiser before she got injured," I explain. Elle had given it to me last night. "But it seems to me that this woman just spent all her time decorating a dumb binder instead of planning."

"That actually sounds like something we would do," Becca says with a grin.

"Yeah, but not anymore. I only have a couple weeks to plan this thing and it's going to be amazing."

The inside pocket of the binder has a checkbook. Elle had explained that there's a five-thousand-dollar budget to throw this banquet. I can pay for the event using these checks. That feels like a really small amount of money to plan something that's supposed to hold one hundred and fifty people. And to make it even scarier, the fundraiser has to earn back at least the five thousand dollars and then more, or otherwise it's not a fundraiser, it's just a money-waster.

The first page in the binder has the previous locations of the fundraiser banquets. Most have been held at the Lawson Community Hall, and a few were held at other facilities in nearby towns. The woman who had this binder before me had handwritten the note "places farther away have less turnout", which leads me to believe I should keep it located here in Lawson.

While Becca and our new temporary employee

handle our first customers of the day, I head to Jace's office in the back of the building and call the Community Hall and ask them about reserving a night for the banquet. What the woman on the other end of the hall tells me makes my jaw drop to the floor. It's three thousand dollars to rent out the facility for one night! That's more than half of my budget! And I'd still have to pay for catering and all the other things that go with hosting an event of this size.

I somehow manage to find the words to thank the woman for her time and tell her I'll let her know if I need to schedule it. Determined not to let this throw me off, I look up every other event facility I can find within a fifteen mile radius. An hour later, I am slouched in Jace's office hair, head in my hands.

Several of the facilities I called don't have any openings any time soon, and furthermore, they're all vastly more expensive than three thousand dollars. It looks like we have to book the Lawson Community Hall, which only gives me two thousand dollars for everything else. I can't just serve basic food—it needs to be quality food. A real, catered dinner, according to the binder. I also need to rent tables and chairs since the facility doesn't have their own, hire an entertainer for the night, a

DJ to play music, and get all the silent auction items. And while the other PTA ladies didn't exactly say this, they do expect me to add a new, exciting flare to the event to draw in more people.

All on two thousand dollars.

I sit up and look around Jace's office, wondering momentarily if I could somehow use The Track as our facility instead so I can save money. But it would be impossible. Our main building is way too small. We could try to do something outside, but it's hot and humid in our part of Texas, and making our guests sweat all evening is no way to throw a proper fundraiser. I have to rent the community hall. Grudgingly, I call back the woman and schedule the rental. She tells me to mail my payment via check within three days to secure my spot. I thank her, write the stupid check, and then lean backward in my chair.

Well, the facility is rented. It's better than nothing. I'll just have to figure out the rest.

My phone buzzes.

I sit up straight when I see Elle's name on the screen.

Elle: Hey girl! I need to go over the official PTA paperwork and handbook with you. Mind if I stop by your house real quick?

My eyes bug out of my head. Elle wants to come to my house? It's not even close to being ready for someone like her to see it! But what am I supposed to do, say no?

I type out a quick reply, telling her I'd love to see her, and then I scramble out of my chair, grab the binder, and run all the way back to my house. Luckily, my living room looks okay. It's the main room I've decorated so far. And the foyer is also good. The whole house smells nice because of my new vanilla-scented candles, so maybe if I can just keep her in the living room, she won't see that the rest of my house is total crap.

In the kitchen, I grab a decorative pitcher and pour a store-bought bottle of sweet tea into it. Then I take out chocolate chip cookies from the package and arrange them on a plate. I bring the whole thing to the coffee table so that I have something to offer her when she visits. Elle always posts online about the importance of hospitality.

I do a quick clean of the hallway bathroom in case she has to pee, turn on the scent warmer in there to make it cozy, and then I change clothes, throwing on a cute white sundress and doing my best "messy bun" that still looks cute the way Elle always has her hair. It's not exactly that cute, but it's better than nothing. I dab on some makeup and take deep breaths in the mirror.

Before I know it, the doorbell rings. Elle is here.

THIRTEEN

THE FIRST THING I notice is the white Range Rover in my driveway. That's a super expensive car. The kind of car that tells everyone you're important. The second thing I notice is Elle's massive hair. She's got her honey-brown locks teased into a big puffy bun that might look weird anywhere else in the world, but it makes her look right at home here in the country. She smells like floral perfume.

"Hey!" she says brightly.

"Come on in." I stand back and let this famous social media influencer into my home. My nerves are working on overdrive here. I feel like she's judging me—and therefore my mom skills—with every passing second. The thing about Elle is that she's super nice, and I'm not sure if she's genuinely nice or if she's one of those judgmental people who only pretend to be nice. I really hope it's the first one. She seems so cool and like she has her life all together.

"Sorry my house is such a mess," I say, lying through my teeth because it's cleaner than it's ever been. "We just moved in not too long ago and I'm still getting it sorted." Technically, it's been a few years, but she doesn't know that. If she thinks I haven't lived here very long, maybe she'll lower her expectations of me.

Maybe she doesn't even have any expectations of me, but still, I want to impress her.

"Oh, it's no worry at all," she says, waving her hand at me as we walk inside. "You have such a cute little home."

My house is two stories tall and not very little in my opinion… which makes me wonder just how massive her house is. It looks immaculate on social media. Maybe it's more of a mansion than a regular house.

I walk quickly from the foyer to the living room, hoping she won't notice any other parts of the house except the one that's slightly nice-looking.

"Want some tea?" I offer, gesturing toward the coffee table. "It's extra sweet."

"I'd love some," she says, taking a seat on the couch. "The only good tea is extra sweet tea."

"It's the Texas way," I say with a smile. At least that part I don't have to fake. We love our sweet tea here.

"Oh, cookies too!" she says, reaching over and taking one. "You're an angel."

I sit next to her, still a little shell-shocked that the famous LawsonMomLife is sitting in my living room. It occurs to me that I've never told her I know she's the famous LawsonMomLife. Maybe I shouldn't mention it now, so I don't look like some weirdo fangirl.

Elle's designer handbag is huge, and she sets it on the floor then pulls out a manilla envelope. She takes out the first set of papers, which is an information sheet I need to fill out. I skim over it, and it's pretty simple. Just my name, info, kid's info, and what skills I can bring to the PTA, along with my availability.

"You can just bring this back to our next meeting if you want," she says. "There's no rush. And then this one is the manual." She hands me a stack of papers that are stapled together. The title page says it's the Parent-Teacher Association Handbook.

"Wow, this is a big handbook," I say, flipping through it. It feels bigger than the one the school gave me when I enrolled Jett.

"It's not a big deal." She takes a bite of cookie and waves her hand to prove her point. "Just standard stuff about being in a group like this. There's also a fairly new ethics page that says don't sleep with any male teachers or a fellow PTA member's husband."

My eyes widen.

She chuckles. "Yeah, that was a whole thing a couple of years ago. But you don't seem like the type to steal someone's husband."

"Definitely not," I say.

Her expression gets softer and she grins. "Of course, you're married to Jace Adams. I don't think you could ever possibly want another man. What's not to love about Jace?" She wiggles her eyebrows at me.

I'm used to women acting like this about my husband, but they're usually women in the motocross world.

"Do any of your kids ride dirt bikes?" I ask, deciding to change the subject a bit.

She shakes her head. "Goodness, no. I think my oldest would love to, but I'm way too scared to let him on a scary machine like that. Your husband is very brave."

"I'm the brave one because I have to sit here and hope he doesn't get hurt each day," I say with a snort.

"That you are," she says. "Being a wife and mother is a full time job. Anyhow, let me dive into this PTA stuff and get it over with."

She goes over the entire handbook with me, skimming over most things, but giving me the basic gist of it all. In addition to the rule of not sleeping with anyone's spouse, we're also expected to act in a way that is appropriate as members of the PTA. We're not supposed to get rip-roaring drunk at functions, or cuss people out, that kind of thing. I'm pretty sure I'll be just fine in that arena.

We also have to attend every single meeting unless there's a valid excuse not to attend, in which case we have to text the PTA president—Elle—beforehand. That seems a little extreme to me, especially since it's a volunteer position, but what-ever. Elle tells me the benefits of being a member outweigh all the rules and standards because the biggest benefit of being in the PTA is the gossip. Apparently, the PTA knows all the gossip before everyone else does.

I have to admit, it's petty of me, but that part sounds fun. I'd love to be kept in the loop of what's going on at my kid's school, and the town in general.

Everything is going great, and I think I'm making a good impression on her. Then the front door opens and Jace and Jett walk inside. In the distance, I hear the screech of the school bus, driving down the road.

"Oh my gosh, I didn't realize how late it was!" I say, glancing at my watch.

But Elle's not paying attention to me. She's staring at Jace with the sweetest, nicest smile ever on her face.

"Hi there," Jace says, nodding in Elle's direction as he takes Jett's backpack off and hangs it up on the hook by the door.

Elle stands up and holds out her hand. "Hello. Jace, right? I'm Elle. It's so nice to meet you."

"Nice to meet you too," he says, shaking her hand. He gives me a quick glance that only me, as his wife understands. It means: *who the heck is this woman?*

"I'm having a little PTA initiation," I say, my voice inflection slightly higher as I realize I'm trying to talk the friendly way Elle does. I feel like a fraud, so I go back to my normal voice. "Paperwork and stuff."

"I'm hungry!" Jett says, tugging at his dad's shirt.

"Oh crap, I forgot to make your snack," I say. "I didn't realize how late it was."

"We were having a great talk," Elle says, still watching Jace. "Your wife is an absolute treasure."

"I think that every day," he says. It makes my knees a little weak.

"I'll go make him a snack," Jace tells me.

"Oh no," Elle says. "Surely, Bayleigh would be happy to do it. It's my fault your snack isn't ready, little man," she says, bending down a bit to look at Jett. "I was keeping Mommy busy, and we lost track of time."

"It's okay," Jett says.

I am momentarily panicked. If I go make Jett a snack, she'll probably follow me into the kitchen. And the kitchen, while clean, is not even close to being decorated to Elle standards. She'll realize I'm a big fraud and not the cool, amazing mother I'm pretending to be. I give Jace a pleading look.

"Mommy needs a break," he says, patting Jett on the shoulder. "Let's go find something to snack on before dinner."

"That's so sweet," Elle says, looking at me. "I'm sure you've got something delicious whipped up for dinner."

I sigh. "I kind of forgot about that, too, actually. I've been so busy all day with the fundraiser banquet and—"

"I'll order takeout," Jace says. "Pizza sounds good. Yeah?"

"Sure—" I say, but I'm interrupted by Elle's shocked gasp.

"Oh goodness gracious," Elle says, hand covering her mouth. "That's awful!"

It doesn't escape my notice when she glances back over at Jace and says, "My man would never be left without a meal. But, that's just how I am. I like to take very good care of him." She reaches over and squeezes my hand. "That's okay, honey. You're young. But you love your husband, so you'll figure it out soon."

FOURTEEN

OUR LIVES HAVE CHANGED SO MUCH NOW that Jett is in school. Partly because now my son goes away for several hours a day when I'm used to him being in the childcare room at work, just a short hallway walk away. I used to eat lunch with him every day and see him when work was slow, and now I don't. That change was inevitable. Your kids can't stay little kids forever. But the other changes are all my doing. Our house being decorated and organized, Jett's lunch kits filled with cute, healthy foods, home-cooked meals, and me making an effort to look nicer each day.

The weird thing is, no one really notices. Jace has said the new house decorations look nice, but I don't think he really cares about them. Jett scarfs down his lunch each day, but I'm pretty sure he'd eat anything I gave him, not caring if his fruits are cut into cute shapes or not. And yet here I am, exhausted each day after getting them ready for work and school and then spending an hour doing my hair and makeup. Still, it's all a sacrifice I'm happy to make to become the best wife and mother I can be.

I still feel a bit like an imposter when I get ready each day, like I'm still some slummy loser under-neath all the glamour and effort I'm making. I'd much rather work in yoga pants and T-shirts, but making myself look nice is a better way to present myself to the world. It tells the world I've got my life together.

The fundraiser banquet is in one week. All the PTA ladies have gushed praise over how incredibly gorgeous the invitations I sent out were. And they were stunning. The invitations were practically wedding-level nice. No one could believe I got something so elegant with my limited budget, and I wasn't about to tell them my trick because I want them to keep me around.

It happened almost on accident. I had spent the day researching the cheapest invitations I could find, but the cheap ones were all so cheesy and simple. I have a list of the 150 honored guests the PTA invites to the banquet each year, most of them business owners and wealthy locals, and as I skimmed over the list of names, one stood out to me. Patricia Brooks, the owner of the stationery store in town.

I got myself all dressed up and then drove over to her shop. I explained that I was looking for something affordable, given my very limited small-town PTA budget, and Patricia offered to do the invitations for free, so long as she could put her logo on the back.

I told her she should include the words "This invitation was donated by" above her logo and she beamed, saying that was a great idea. Now her company gets the good will and free advertising and we get free invitations in return. Since the venue costs three thousand dollars, leaving me only two thousand for everything else, I decided to see if I could use the same technique with other vendors.

All my catering food quotes were for twenty five dollars a person, which is more than twice the money I had to spend on it. So instead of using the big corporate companies that my predecessor had written in her binder, I called up local restaurants and asked if they can do catering for a smaller budget since it's a school fundraiser. The third company I called—a delicious Mexican restaurant—offered to do it for their cost only, which was significantly cheaper at five dollars a person. To thank them for their generosity, I promised to include their name on our wall of heroes – which is a thing I made up on the spot.

Now, I have this cool banner that was printed up at a local print shop for free that says Wall of Heroes, along with the business names of everyone who donated. When I told Elle about my technique of asking if people can donate toward our fundraiser instead of making us pay full cost, she was ecstatic. She said she couldn't believe no one had thought of that before.

So even though I've never even been to a fundraiser banquet, I think I've planned a pretty kick-ass event. We'll have dinner catered, a local bluegrass band performing for tips only (because the band members are all parents or grandparents of Lawson Elementary schools and they were happy to volunteer their time), over a hundred silent auction items that were donated, tables and chairs also donated, tablecloths and floral centerpieces donated to us from a local florist, and the high school ROTC kids offered to be ushers for the night, helping our guests with anything they need.

As it turns out, I am under budget. I'm so thrilled I could burst. This is my first PTA event and I am absolutely killing it.

Around noon, a delivery driver drops off the new wall shelves I ordered for my bedroom. Since I'm still off work, I take a break from banquet planning to assemble and install the shelves. Jace usually does stuff like this for me, but part of being an awesome wife is knowing how to use power tools yourself like a badass.

It only takes a little effort and now I have really nice shelves which I fill with framed pictures and a few sentimental knickknacks. After making my bed, vacuuming the floor, and dusting the furniture, I check my email and see that someone has reached out to me regarding the banquet.

She's the owner of a party business that provides big balloon decorations, like those giant numbers filled with balloons that people get for their birthdays. She said she heard from some other local business that the school is having a fundraiser and she wants to donate a LAWSON ELEMEN-TARY balloon sign to display on the stage at the banquet hall as well as a balloon arch for the entryway.

All for free. I squeal excitedly and quickly type out a reply email, thanking her so much for her generous donation. I need to measure the stage so I can give her accurate sizing info, and I also need to check out some things at the event hall anyway so I can finalize my table placement chart and make sure the area I have planned for the silent auction will have enough room.

On my way to the banquet hall, tape measure in hand, I see Jace standing outside near The Track's main building, so I pull in and say hello.

"Hey there, beautiful," he says, walking up to me. He's wearing his standard work uniform, which is motocross boots, riding pants, and no shirt. I'm pretty fond of this uniform.

"I'm on my way to measure the banquet hall."

"Have I told you you've done an amazing job on this?" he says, leaning into my driver's side car window.

"Yes, but you can say it again."

He leans in and kisses me. "You're doing an amazing job on this."

I grin. "Thanks, babe."

On the short drive to the banquet hall, I'm

dancing in my car to some pop music. I know my house still needs a little work, and my cooking skills are improving but not perfect, but I've totally got this whole life thing figured I'm doing a great job, and it's all thanks to meeting Elle and stalking her social media.

The Lawson Community Hall is a multi-purpose building that several organizations use for all kinds of things. People even have weddings here. The large building looks plain from the outside, with its tan concrete walls and large parking lot, but inside it can be made to look beautiful.

There's no one here today which is good news because I should be able to slip inside and take my measurements without disturbing anyone. When I try to open the door, it's locked. There's a door bell to the side, so I press it and wait.

A woman in a bright red shirt opens the door, smiling at me. "Hello, how can I help you?"

I recognize her voice as the person I spoke to on the phone when I reserved the facility. I hold up my tape measure. "Hi, I was hoping to come take some measurements of the banquet hall for my decorators."

"What's your name?"

"Bayleigh Adams."

She frowns. "Ah, yes, Mrs. Adams. Have you chosen another date for your event?"

"No, what do you mean? I want the same date I scheduled."

She gives me a concerned look that makes my insides instantly tense up. "No, I'm sorry but we never received your payment so we had to give the date to someone else."

"What?" My voice is so shocked it doesn't even sound like me. "That can't be true."

"I'm sorry, Mrs. Adams, but you never paid."

"Yes, I did. I remember writing the check."

"Okay…" she says, quirking an eyebrow. "But did you ever mail it?"

FIFTEEN

THIS CAN'T BE HAPPENING. I speed through town, panic flushing through my entire body making me sweat and hyperventilate. Once I get home, I burst through the door and run to the dining room where I'd left the banquet planning binder. I'm going to get the check number, call the bank, and verify that the banquet hall cashed my check. Then I'll demand that they give us the date we reserved.

Only…

As I open the binder, I see the check. The three thousand dollar check that I wrote, tore out of the checkbook, and stuffed in an envelope. It even has a stamp on it.

But I never mailed it. I completely forgot to mail it.

How could I have been so stupid?

I try taking calming breaths, but they don't help. I am freaking out. My hands shake as I call the Lawson Community Hall and the same woman answers.

"Lawson Community Hall."

"Hi, this is Bayleigh Adams."

"Mmhmm?" She says it in this petty way, like she knows I've realized my mistake. And she's right.

"I'm so sorry, but you were right. I just found the check that never got mailed. It was in an envelope and everything, and I don't know how this happened."

"Well, that's a shame, but I'm happy to book another date for you if we have one available."

"I really need this date, ma'am," I plead into the phone. "Is there any way I can reserve the hall for this date?"

"No, it's already been reserved and paid for. We operate on a first come, first served basis."

"What if I pay you five thousand dollars instead of three?"

She chuckles. "This is a city property and there are rules. We can't just auction off our hall to the highest bidder. I can check the calendar and find another date for you."

"No, I can't use another date. The invitations have already been mailed out." I'm pacing back and forth, feeling like I could pass out at any moment.

The woman chuckles. "Oh, that is unfortunate. Hopefully you didn't invite too many people."

Tears burst from my eyes. "Please," I say. "Is there anything I can do? Can you please, please, help me out here? What if I rented a giant tent and just used your parking lot that way the address is the same?"

"Then where would my other reservation's guests park? Seriously, Mrs. Adams. You need to take some responsibility and solve your own problems. There's nothing I can do for you."

And with that, she hangs up.

I hear the sound of the school bus screeching to a stop in front of our house and I walk out there on autopilot, smiling at my son as he steps off the bus even though I don't feel happy at all.

"How was school?" I ask, sounding like a zombie.

"It was fun." Jett holds my hand as we walk back inside. "I'm hungry."

"Sit at the table and I'll make you a snack."

My heart aches as I chop up some strawberries for Jett. I feel like I'm in a daze, walking around my house in a blur. I have screwed up so badly. Not only is this a big deal, it's also a betrayal of the school. My kid's school depends on these fundraisers to give the students happier, more enriched school lives. I can't believe I'm letting them all down like this.

Tears well up in my eyes again and I hold them back. I can't let my son see me crying or then he'll know I'm a failure.

"Mommy?" Jett says from the kitchen table.

"Yes?" I blink back tears and look over at him, putting on my best smile.

"You look pretty today."

He stares at me with all the sincerity in the world, and now those tears come right back.

I ruffle his hair. "Thank you, baby."

Jace texts me after work and asks if he can stay later and joyride dirt bikes with Park. I would laugh if I wasn't so stressed out because he does not need to ask me permission to do anything. He's just nice like that I guess. I text him back and say that's fine with me because I have something to do with Becca.

Now I hope Becca has some free time because I could really use her.

Jett and I walk over to her house. She's only been off work for half an hour, and her car is in the driveway, but she doesn't answer when I knock on the door. Jett runs to the porch swing and starts swinging on it while I wait, and wait. I send her a text but she doesn't reply. That usually means one thing—either she's in the shower or she's painting.

I let myself in with my copy of her house key.

"Hello?" I call out. "It's me!"

"And me!" Jett says beside me.

I don't see anything, but there is a subtle music thumping from upstairs. My suspicions were correct. I jog up three flights of stairs to the small but adorable painting studio. The door is cracked open a few inches and I see Becca facing the large window, a half-painted canvas in front of her.

"Hello," I call out.

She turns around, smiling when she sees me. "Hey!"

She turns off the music. "What's up?"

I put a hand on Jett's shoulder. "Honey, will you go watch TV in the living room?"

His eyes light up. "Yes!"

Lately I've been making him do some chores around the house right after school. Nothing serious, just simple things like helping me load the dishwasher. LawsonMomLife says teaching kids how to do chores early on is a good thing.

"What's wrong?" Becca whispers after Jett goes downstairs.

I start crying, which makes it hard to talk. The only words I manage are, "I've totally screwed up."

"With what?" she says, pulling me into a hug. "Honey, it can't be too bad. What is it?"

"It's really, really bad."

Concern flashes across her features and I can tell she's probably picturing every horrible thing in the world right now.

"It's the PTA," I say to set her mind at ease. Yes, this is really bad, but it's not like I robbed a bank or anything.

She relaxes a bit, then pulls me into her kitchen and pours two cups of sweet tea.

"What happened?"

I take a shuddering breath, grateful Jett is fully entertained by the television right now so he won't see his mom looking like a total loser. Then I explain everything to my best friend. She listens, but she doesn't panic.

"It's okay," she says, holding out her hands on the table. "We'll fix this."

"How are we possibly going to fix it? The invitations went out with an address of a place we don't have reserved!"

"We'll just send new invitations," she says. "And we'll find a new place."

"Not only are new invitations going to cost a lot of money, what happens when someone gets a new invitation with a totally different information? They'll think I'm an idiot!"

"So what," Becca says with a wave of her hand. "We'll make the new invitations say there's been a change of plans. Maybe we'll give them an extra door prize or something for the hassle. It'll be fine."

I admire her enthusiasm, and it's actually starting to make me feel better, too.

"Okay." I swallow the lump in my throat. "I guess."

"Cool." She smiles then takes a long sip of her drink. "Oh! I have an idea. Why don't we have it here?"

"At your house?" I say sarcastically. "There's not enough room."

"No, I mean at the track. We can set it up outside."

I shake my head. "The PTA wants it indoors because it's too hot outside and too nasty, according to some of our highest donors. They want to dine and relax in luxury."

Becca blows a raspberry with her tongue. "Fine. If they want an indoor party, they'll get an indoor party."

She grabs her iPad from the counter and props it up between us. We search all the same facilities I've already researched. Sure they cost more, but I'm desperate. I need something and I'll just have to pay out of my own pocket if necessary. I can't let the PTA down.

Becca calls some of the facilities and I call the others. But by the time we reach the end of the list, all of that small glimmer of hope I had earlier is gone. Shattered. Dashed. There's not a single facility that has an opening on our scheduled date. I change the search radius to an hour away, hoping there's something somewhere with an opening.

But the only answer I get is no.

I am so screwed.

SIXTEEN

TWO DAYS GO BY. I still haven't figured out what to do, and I know that each day that passes without me confessing how royally I screwed up is only making things worse. I should just suck up my pride and tell Elle that I'm a miserable failure who has ruined the annual fundraiser banquet, and maybe she'll be able to find a way to fix things. She's a woman who has her life together, after all. I'm just the pathetic loser who is pretending to have my life together.

But as each minute passes, I can't seem to make myself call her and admit the truth. I have this futile feeling deep in the pit of my stomach that keeps thinking I might find a way to pull this off.

And that's the dumbest feeling I've ever had. I

can't pull this off. There's just no way. Invitations have already been mailed out. Invitations that direct everyone to a time and place where our event won't be. I can't backtrack from this. I'm going to ruin my reputation. And Jace's too, by extension. We'll be known as the couple who ruined the Lawson Elementary fundraiser. Our business might even suffer from the blowback.

Oh no. I'm going to be sick.

The bathroom is too far away. I fling open the back door and run as far as I can into the grass before I puke. The only thing in my stomach is about three cups of coffee and it burns coming back up. I'm a shaky, nervous, wreck.

I stand up after a few moments and take a deep breath as tears pool in my eyes. I don't know what to do. Today is the last day of my week off work, and I'll be stuck going back tomorrow. If I can't fix it today, it'll never get fixed.

I go back inside and brush my teeth and drink some water even though I still feel sick with worry. An idea comes to me. I don't think Jace would like it. But I could just donate several thousand dollars to the school myself. Elle had said the PTA usually raises about around seven to ten thousand dollars each year. Maybe I can just give our own savings money to them and apologize for ruining the banquet.

Or maybe I should return all the home décor I bought and use that money. I don't deserve a nice home if I can't even be trusted to run a banquet. Tears fill my eyes at the thought, but I make a decision right there, right now, in my living room. If I can't fix the banquet in twenty four hours, I'll donate all the money myself. Jace will be upset, but he loves me and he'll find a way to get over it. I hope.

I take a shower and cry a bit, and then I force myself to get dressed and compose myself. I can't lose all hope now, even though it still feels pretty hopeless. I eat some toast to calm my nausea, and then drive into town. I go straight to the Community Hall. There's an event going on this morning, some kind of craft fair judging by the signs outside, so the door is unlocked and open.

I let myself inside, looking around at all the booths. Making my way across the large room, I find a hallway off to the side. I'm not exactly sure what my plan is, but I'm hoping to find the woman in charge and then somehow sweet-talk her into letting me have the phone number of whoever has reserved this hall on the date of the fundraiser.

I walk all over, keeping an eye out for her, but I never see her. I do, however, find a closed office doorway in the back of the hallway. The little plaque on the door says this office belongs to the event coordinator. I peer in through the thin, narrow window and see the office is empty.

I bite my lip. Looking both directions, I confirm that I'm all alone in this tiny hallway that's only meant for employees. I try my luck and decide to touch the doorknob. It's unlocked. My heart races. Am I seriously about to break into someone's office?

The door quietly opens and I slip inside.

Apparently, I *am* going to break into someone's office.

The only sound I hear is the powerful thudding in my chest. I don't even know what I'm looking for until I see it. The black, leather bound binder sits on the middle of her desk. She looked through it back when I first talked to her about renting the space. Quickly, I rush over and flip it open. I turn to this month and flip to the date that was supposed to be my fundraiser date. With any luck, it'll have the name and number of who reserved it and I can call them and beg them to give me their date.

I find the name and my heart drops. It isn't a

regular person. It's not some small business who could easy reschedule their event.

Nope.

It's Marci Blackwell.

A Texas senator. The most popular, most loved senator of the state.

Defeated, I close the book and rush out of the office, leaving everything exactly as I found it. The hallway is still empty so my crime won't be noticed. I walk back out to my car, not even finding the energy to look around at all the craft booths that I would normally love under any other circumstance.

On my phone, I Google Marci Blackwell's website and find that she's scheduled her own political fundraiser for the date. It'll be a huge event with lots of her wealthy donors attending. She's no doubt spent tons more money advertising her event than we did on ours, and there's no way I can convince her to change her mind. It's not even worth trying. A small town school PTA can't compete with a freaking senator.

I clench my fists and let out a frustrated groan in my car. Tears spring to my eyes as I drive back home, wishing I had a way to fix this problem. Wishing I hadn't been so forgetful in the first place.

All I had to do was mail the check and this would have been prevented.

At home, I don't bother doing any of the chores I had planned to do. I have some décor items still in boxes. Some cleaning still needing to be done. I even bought a new curling iron to try out new hair-styles and I can't be bothered to play with it now. I just sit on the couch and wallow in pity and shame.

When Jett gets home, I make him a snack and then let him watch TV because I can't seem to get the energy I need to play games or do anything fun with him right now. It feels like my life is a ticking clock, counting down to the moment when I have to reveal my failures to everyone.

When Jace gets off work, I decide to scrape myself together and make some dinner. I might as well do one final good thing before I have to come clean about my epic screw up. I decide to make cheeseburgers, only I get distracted by attempting to toast the buns on the stove that I let my stupid burger patties burn.

I curse under my breath and pull them off the stove, hoping they'll still be edible even though they're a little blacker than they should be. Jace walks in the back door and plants a kiss on my forehead.

"Smells good," he says as he walks to the fridge and grabs a soda.

"It won't be good," I mutter as I set out three plates and make three burgers. "I burned the meat."

"Nah, it's just a little crispy," Jace says. He's in such a good mood it makes me want to roll my eyes. Of course he can be in a good mood... he didn't ruin his child's fundraiser. I did. And I don't know how I'm supposed to tell him.

While I set the table for dinner, Jace makes sure our son washes his grubby hands before sitting at the table. While they eat, I listen to Jett tell us about his day at school and all of his friends, and how he thinks some of the girls are weird because they always want to sit by him.

"That just means they like you," Jace says.

Jett curls his lip. "Well, they're weird."

Even I laugh at this, even though I'm holding back a tidal wave of stress. I watch my little family eat the burnt dinner I made them without complaint, and I try to cherish these last few minutes before everything goes to hell.

SEVENTEEN

I'M BACK at work today. Of course with my luck, The Track is busier than usual, since Park and Jace scheduled several back-to-back large training sessions. We have thirty teenagers here to get lessons today. They're so serious about the sport that they've even taken off school for the day. Some of the kids are homeschooled specifically so they have more time to ride dirt bikes. Our front office is a mad house right now and Becca and I are working hard to keep up with signing in everyone, taking their payments, and processing their paperwork.

The good thing about being ridiculously busy is that it takes my mind off the drama with the PTA fundraiser. The bad thing is that it only helps a little. Even while I'm working my butt off at the front desk, I still have this nagging horrible feeling in my chest that reminds me I'll have to call Elle and the rest of the PTA and tell them their new member ruined the banquet.

I've thought everything over in my mind. There is no fix. The best I could do is try to host the event here at The Track, but it's a dirty dirt pit here. Which is great for dirt bikes because they're made for dirt. A fancy banquet would be so out of place here!

Even if I found some way to decorate the outside, it would still look crummy. I can't even bring myself to offer The Track as a solution when I have to tell Elle. She's a glamorous, beautiful woman with a clean house and designer clothes. She won't want our fancy deep-pocketed donors to go to a dirt bike track fundraiser. She'll probably laugh in my face and then banish me from the PTA forever. I might even get banned from ever volunteering in Lawson ISD ever again. The thought makes me want to cry.

But I'm at work, so I suck it up and get back to work.

By the time I get a little break, I slump into my stool behind the front counter and open my phone. I have several notifications from all the accounts I follow online and a few email subscriptions I signed up for. These are all from the new life I wanted to create for myself. How to cook dinners, how to style my hair, how to keep a clean house. All of these sites provide information for someone who deserves to be the best wife and mother around. Right now, I'm not feeling like any of that is true. I am a failure, plain and simple.

I clear out the notifications and stare at my phone. My phone wallpaper is a picture of Jace, Jett, and me at the beach last summer. I wish I could close my eyes and transport myself back into that day so I could live the last few months all over again and do them the right way.

As I'm staring at my phone, a text appears. It's from Elle, and my heart sinks seeing her name on the screen. Reluctantly, I click on it.

Elle: Girlllll!!! I am freaking out!

My heart skips a beat. If she's freaking out, maybe she already knows? Maybe someone told her I never booked our venue? My heart races and my palms feel sweaty. Even my back feels sweaty. I'm so not ready to face the consequences right now, but if she already knows, then at least I don't have to tell her. I can't think of anything to reply back right now, and it takes me too long to think of something before she's texting me again.

Elle: you will never believe this… but…

Elle: We had a 100% YES to our RVSPs!!!!!!!! Every single person has agreed to come! I was afraid we'd be scrambling last minute to fill empty seats but now we don't have to. YAY!

Elle: we're going to raise so much money!

With each new text that comes in, my dread grows stronger. Breaking the bad news to her will be a million times harder now. Plus it means I'll have to call every single person we invited and tell them that the event is over. Oh god. This is going to suck. I almost feel like throwing up again.

My thumb hovers over the phone screen. I need to reply. Normally I would have already replied. Up until I ruined the fundraiser, I thought getting texts from

Elle was the coolest thing ever and I always rushed to reply to her. Now I wish I had never met her. Never got involved with the PTA. Never agreed to host a banquet despite having no idea what I'm doing. Now I wish I could go back in time and change everything

"You okay?" Becca says, nudging my back as she walks by.

"Yeah," I manage to say.

She disappears down the hallway and returns a few minutes later with a stack of envelopes and stamps. "You look freaked out," she says. Then her brows pull together. "Oh crap. I almost forgot. The venue thing. Is it fixed?"

Besides that one night I asked her to help me find a new venue, I've kept Becca and everyone else in my life in the dark about what's going on. I know Becca is my best friend and will support me no matter what, but it's just so embarrassing to let her know how badly I screwed up.

Before I can answer her, a client enters the front office. Becca steps up and helps them sign in. I look back at my phone, realize I have no idea what to say to Elle, and set it back down on the counter.

After the customer has left, Becca turns to me. "So what new venue did you find?"

I shrug. "I didn't."

"So you got the other person to cancel their reservation for your original date?"

I shrug again. "Nope."

"So are you changing the date or something?"

I shake my head.

She frowns. "I don't understand."

I take a ragged breath and rest my head in my hands. I'm quiet for a long moment, and I think Becca is starting to realize what this means. Finally, I look up and into my best friend's eyes.

"I failed. I don't know what to do. There is nothing to do. I completely, totally, failed."

"Oh no, honey," she says, hugging me. "It's not a failure. We can fix this."

I snort out a laugh. "No, we can't. There's no way to fix it. If there was, I would have figured it out by now. And now I'll have to tell Elle, and she'll tell the whole PTA, and every member and every person we invited, and the entire town is going to hate me. I've ruined everything."

Becca takes my hand and squeezes it. "Bayleigh."

When I don't look up, she says my name again. "Hey. You. Look at me."

I roll my eyes and then drag my face up to hers. She smiles. "You need to tell Jace."

I snort. "Hell no."

"Yes, tell him. He'll know what to do."

I shake my head. Above me, the whir of the air conditioning fills the room. And beyond that, the gentle sound of dirt bikes fills the air, a sound I've come to know and love. It's the sound of home. And safety. And our livelihood. It's a sound that used to comfort me, and now I'm here feeling like nothing will ever be okay again.

"I can't tell Jace," I say, shaking my head. "I mean, I know he'll find out eventually, but I don't want to bother him with it right now. I've spent the last few weeks trying to be the best wife and mom ever, and now I'll just have to admit that I'm a failure."

"So what?" Becca says. Which is kind of weird, because I was expecting her to say I'm not a failure, or something nice like that since that's what best friends do. Instead, she's calling me out on my crap.

"So what," she says again. "Tell Jace what happened. Tell him you forgot to mail the check. He's really smart and he'll do whatever it takes to fix this."

"I don't want to rely on my husband for everything," I mutter. "I want to do things myself. I want to show him, and everyone else, that being a young mother isn't a bad thing. I want to be competent. And yet, despite all my efforts, I'm not."

"I get that, Bay. I really do." She smiles at me. "But you're not just a wife and mother. You're a partner. And your other half is Jace, and he took wedding vows and promised to be there for you. You two are a team, and if anyone can help, it'll be him. You need to ask him."

I bite my lip so hard I taste blood.

Maybe she's right.

EIGHTEEN

THE TRACK GETS busy again shortly after my conversation with Becca, so I'm able to temporarily pretend my problems don't exist for another couple of hours. I enjoy staying busy, but it doesn't help the knot in my stomach. Eventually the customers stop coming, and before I know it, it's closing time.

"I'll finish up here," Becca says, walking over to the front door and turning off the neon OPEN light. "Why don't you head home early?"

"No, I'll stay and help you close," I say.

She gives me a knowing look. "Or you could go home early and get started on what you need to do."

I grimace.

"I'll even take Jett home from the childcare room and hang out with him for a bit."

"You don't need to do that," I start saying, but then I realize it's actually a good idea. I'll probably start crying when I tell Jace how I screwed up the fundraiser, and it'll be better if Jett isn't around to see it. I suck in air through my teeth. "Okay. Thank you."

I swing by the childcare room and tell Jett he's going to hang out with Aunt Becca for a little bit. He's happy because he loves going over to their house and getting spoiled rotten. I give him a goodbye kiss and then head out the back door, glancing around for Jace.

He's chatting with a client's dad, and waves when he sees me standing here. I absolutely hate that I'm about to tell him about my failure. I kind of wish I could run away instead.

I wait until the client leaves, and then Jace walks toward me, grinning that cute little grin of his.

"Hey beautiful," he says. He always says that. I don't feel very beautiful right now. I feel like the world's biggest loser.

"Hey." My throat feels dry. Normally we'd walk inside and get Jett from the childcare room, or he'd already be with me. "Becca is hanging out with Jett for a while," I explain.

"Cool. We could go get dinner or something and celebrate being childless for a bit?"

I shrug. Food doesn't sound good right now.

"What's wrong? You look like you're sick or something."

"Kind of," I say.

"What are your symptoms?" he says, jumping into problem-fixing mode. His hand touches my forehead. "Do you have a fever?"

"I'm not sick like that," I say, staring down at the grass beneath us. "I'm sick in an emotional way."

His arm slips around me. "Talk to me," he says softly as we start walking toward our house.

Several seconds pass and I'm not sure how to get the words out. After all, this is my thing that I screwed up. It doesn't really affect him the same way. He'll probably just shrug and tell me to get over it and move on and let it go. Jace doesn't care if I'm in the PTA or not.

But I care. And I wanted to be the perfect mom.

We're all the way to our back porch before I can speak. And when I find the words, they just tumble out of me.

"I forgot to mail the check to book the community hall for the banquet and they gave the date to someone else, the senator, and I've called everywhere around here and can't find another venue to have the banquet, and plus the invitations have already been sent out saying it's taking place at the community hall, when it's not, and the entire PTA is going to hate me, but especially Elle, and I can't believe I'm so stupid! And I should have told Elle by now and I just can't. I've put it off until the last possible moment and I hate myself so much."

Jace's eyes open wide as I let all this word vomit spew out of me unchecked and frantic. When I finally stop talking, I feel an immense relief. I mean, I'm still a total failure, but at least my husband knows now. One of the hard parts is over. Next, I have to tell Elle.

Jace's lips press into a line and his eyes focus somewhere off in the distance. It's his thinking look. The seconds tick on and I'm standing here watching him with curiosity and impatience. I wish he would talk.

"Well?" I say, nudging his shoe with my foot. "Aren't you going to tell me what a loser I am?"

He grins, then reaches out and touches my

cheek. "Babe, you're not a loser. Not in any possible way."

"I am a loser, in a huge, mega huge way."

He shakes his head. "No, you're not. You're just stressed. You've been working really hard, and you made one simple mistake and that kind of thing happens to everyone. No one is perfect."

I groan and roll my eyes. "I should have been perfect."

"Baby…" Jace takes both of my hands in his and leans down until our foreheads touch. "Why didn't you tell me sooner?"

I shrug. "I wanted to do this all on my own. I didn't want to go running to my husband to fix my screw up."

"I guess I can understand that," he says softly, his lips pressing to my forehead. "But you shouldn't keep everything to yourself. You should tell me."

"I didn't want to stress you out, too. I kept thinking maybe I could fix this. I thought I *should* fix it. I'm trying to be perfect, here."

"Perfect is overrated." He pulls me into his arms, and I relax against his chest. It's the safest I've felt in days. "Bayleigh, we're a team," he says, his chin resting on top of my head, his arms tightly around me. "When I have a problem, I go to you.

And when you have a problem, you should come to me. I will always be here for you. Always."

"I know," I mutter softly. Because I do know. Jace is my husband. My partner. My perfect other half. I know I can go to him with anything. I just wish I didn't have to.

He squeezes me before letting me go and peering down at me, his eyes filled with love. "This will be okay, Bayleigh."

"No, it won't. Maybe in fifty years from now I'll finally be able to get over it, but not any time soon."

"You said a senator has already reserved the date you wanted?"

I nod. "Marci Blackwell."

"Okay," he says, deep in thought. "Okay, cool. I think we can fix this."

My chest aches. I can't bring myself to think even for a second that he's serious and that this can be fixed. "How?"

He leans down and kisses me. He tastes like sweat and lemon lime sports drink. When he pulls back, that sneaky little grin of his is exciting and a bit terrifying. When Jace wants to do something, he gets it done. I'm just not sure what he plans to do.

"Let's call the senator."

NINETEEN

JACE HAS A GOOD IDEA, and he knows it, which is why he's being a butt-head and not telling me his great idea. Instead, I watch with wide eyes and a slight optimism as he looks up the number for the senator's office.

We're sitting in the living room, my nice new clean and organized living room. It feels like the décor of an imposter. My phone gets a text.

Becca: How's it going?

Me: He's not mad at me

Becca: Duhhhhhhhhhhhhhhhhhh

Me: He thinks he has an idea to fix everything, but I'm not sure if it'll work

Becca: Keep me updated! Park and Jett are playing video games right now, so take all the time you need.

Me: thanks :)

The next few minutes go by in a blur. First, I'm biting my lip, bouncing my foot, and watching in anxious awe as Jace talks to someone on the other end of the phone. Obviously the senator herself isn't going to answer calls from just anybody, so he's talking to some kind of assistant. Then he's transferred to another assistant. Maybe someone higher up in the chain of command. Then my heart stops when he tells them about our fundraiser date, and what he would like them to do. It's genius. It's brilliant. I can't believe it.

After a few minutes, he's thanking the person on the other end, and hanging up.

"Well?" I say.

He grins. "They agreed."

I bolt off the couch. "They did?"

"Yep."

He's looking very proud of himself right now. A little cocky, even.

I throw myself into his arms, and we fall back

on the couch. "Thank you, thank you," I say, kissing him and crawling onto his lap. "I can't believe you pulled this off."

He kisses my neck and grabs my hips, pulling me against him. "You're so sexy when you're happy like this."

"You made that possible," I say.

"I didn't do it for a reward but…" He wiggles his eyebrows suggestively. "Maybe I can get a reward?"

I laugh, pressing my hands to his chest. "Of course you can. But you need to shower first. You smell like sweat and dirt bike grease."

"Aww, shucks," he says, making a pouting face. "Maybe you can come shower with me?"

I climb off his lap and curl my finger toward him. "Let's go."

After Jace and I spent an amazing, romantic, sweet, loving night together, I wake up the next day energized and feeling like myself again. No, like a better version of myself. Everything is going to be okay. In fact, it's going to be even better than okay.

Jace's plan was to ask the senator if we can both

share the fundraiser night. Her event was scheduled for the afternoon, ending about an hour after we were supposed to start our dinner. Now, her event takes place first, and then leads into our event. After all, what senator wouldn't want the good press that comes with promoting a school fundraiser? It makes her look good and it helps us raise more money.

In return, Jace offered to let her host fundraising events at The Track any time she wants, for free.

To make things even better, the senator herself offered to match our fundraising donations one to one. So for every dollar we raise, she'll match it. This is going to be a huge event for us. And it gives her lots of good press and will make her voters love her even more.

Elle just about loses her mind when I call and tell her the good news. I word it in a way that doesn't reveal how I screwed up the reservations. Instead, I act like it was all part of the plan. I got our venue, negotiated very cheap or free local vendors to help us set it up, and we got a senator on board to help out our fundraiser.

"I am so proud of you!" she says. I can hear her smile through the phone. "Wow, this is amazing. The PTA is going to be so thrilled. I've been telling them we need to bring on more younger members… get some fresh blood in here, ya know? Those old ladies are so boring and uninspired."

I grin. "I'm just happy to be included."

"So what can I help you with before the big day?" she asks.

"Ummm…" I glance at the binder. I know all the details of the fundraiser. All the vendors. All the decorations. It's all set. "I don't really need any help," I admit. "Everything is all set to go."

"You are an angel," she says. "You're an absolute angel."

Later, I'm standing in my closet, looking at all my clothes. Some are older, stuff I've had for years. A lot of it is new. Clothes I bought online after stalking Elle's social media and trying to emulate her style. Almost all of it still has the tags on because I haven't been many places to wear any of it. There are five dresses I bought for the banquet, and I can't decide which one would be the best one to wear. Should I look more formal? Professional?

My eyes are drawn to a maroon sweater dress. It has long puffy sleeves, but fits snug around my body. I could put a belt around the waist. Maybe wear some knee-high leather boots with it. I'm not entirely sure how to style my hair, but maybe some kind of half-up, half-down style? And big hoop earrings? Or drop earrings? Or maybe just my diamond studs. Simple and elegant.

I lose track of time as I stand here and try to choose the perfect outfit. I want something that says I'm mature and responsible and worthy of being the perfect wife and mom.

But you know what? It's kind of exhausting. Sometimes I just want to wear yoga pants and baggy T-shirts I've stolen from Jace, and leave my hair in a messy bun for days, my face clean and free of makeup.

Sometimes I just want to be me.

TWENTY

THE LAWSON COMMUNITY HALL has been transformed. The plain, big empty building is now a fall wonderland of decorations and tables. Beautiful lights give the place a charming glow, and the smell of the catered dinner makes my mouth water. A live band plays music on the stage, which is decorated with my big Lawson Elementary fundraiser banner as well as a smaller banner from Senator Blackwell. Even though the senator is much more important than our little PTA group, she's made an effort to let the school fundraiser have most of the attention tonight. It's a really classy move from her. She even insisted on paying the rental fee for the venue tonight even when I tried to pay it myself, or split the cost with her. Now we're on track to earn three or four times more money than we ever imagined.

I did choose the sweater dress to wear tonight, along with some brown knee-high boots. I didn't do much to my hair, though. I decided I want to live my life as myself. Not as someone else I wish I could be. And sometimes I want to put in a lot of effort, and sometimes I don't. Tonight was a compromise.

As much as I love the LawsonMomLife social media page, maybe that's all I need it to be. A fun source of entertainment that I can look at occasionally. I can take inspiration from Elle's posts whenever I want to, but not try so hard to copy her that it stresses me out. I like my life. Even when it's messy and unorganized. Because even if I'm not the perfect wife and mom, I have the perfect husband and son. It doesn't get any better than that.

I've been here for hours setting up with the other PTA ladies, so Jace brings Jett by to see the fundraiser for a little bit. I was going to leave him with our babysitter, Deja, for the night, but Jace insisted on letting him see what his mom accomplished tonight. Our son's eyes are wide and awed as he looks around at the decorated room filled with people.

Jace has dressed him in a little suit, and he's

the cutest thing ever. Especially standing next to his dad, who is also wearing a suit. My dirt-bike-loving boys can clean up really nicely when they need to.

"What do you think?" I ask, kneeling down to Jett's eye level.

"It looks cool," he says, smiling. "It's kind of girly though."

I laugh. "What would you rather it look like?"

He considers it for a moment. "Monster trucks and dirt bikes."

"Well maybe we can decorate the next event with monster trucks and dirt bikes."

He nods, like this is a really good idea. "Okay, Mommy. I'll help you next time."

I ruffle his hair. "Thank you."

"I'm going to take him back home to Deja," Jace says, holding onto Jett's little hand. "Then when I come back, you're going to dance with me."

My eyes widen. "No one is dancing," I say, glancing toward the band. People are sitting at their tables, mulling around the silent auction tables, and talking with the senator on the other side of the room. But no one is dancing.

"We'll get the party started," Jace says, flashing me a smile.

I roll my eyes. I wish he were joking about danc-ing, but he's probably not.

"Oh, and I almost forgot to tell you," Jace says, pulling an envelope from the inside of his jacket pocket. "I told Tyrone about the fundraiser."

"That guy who works at Exxon?" I ask. He drives an incredibly expensive truck and his sons ride the best of the best dirt bikes. Everything they own is top-of-the-line quality.

"Yep," Jace says, handing the envelope to me. "He wanted to make a donation for the PTA."

I'm giddy with anticipation as I open the enve-lope, hoping he donated a lot. Maybe even a few hundred dollars. But when I see the zeroes on the check, I almost pass out.

"Ten thousand dollars?" I read it again just in case I read it wrong. "Is this for real?"

"Yep," Jace says. "The dude is super rich."

"Oh my gosh. This is amazing. I have to call and thank him." I tuck the check back into the envelope with plans to rush it over to the PTA's bank account ASAP so I don't lose it. "And thank you, babe. We'd never have this money without your help."

"Hey, we're a team," Jace says, kissing me.

Below us, Jett says, "Ewwww."

"You won't think kissing is so gross when you meet the girl of your dreams one day," Jace tells him.

Our son curls his lip. "I don't think so. Girls are gross."

"Oh, trust me," Jace says with a chuckle. He looks up at me. "You might not think so now, but the girl of your dreams will change your life."

ABOUT THE AUTHOR

Amy Sparling is the bestselling author of books for teens and the teens at heart. She lives on the coast of Texas with her family, her spoiled rotten pets, and a huge pile of books. She graduated with a degree in English and has worked at a bookstore, coffee shop, and a fashion boutique. Her fashion skills aren't the best, but luckily she turned her love of coffee and books into a writing career that means she can work in her pajamas. Her favorite things are coffee, book boyfriends, and Netflix binges.

She's always loved reading books from R. L. Stine's Fear Street series, to The Baby Sitter's Club series by Ann, Martin, and of course, Twilight. She started writing her own books in 2010 and now publishes several books a year. Amy loves getting messages from her readers and responds to every single one! Connect with her on one of the links below.

www.AmySparling.com

facebook.com/authoramysparling

bookbub.com/profile/amy-sparling

goodreads.com/Amy_Sparling

Printed in Great Britain
by Amazon